KT-492-786

Cardiff Libraries
www.cardiff.gov.uk/libraries

Llyfrgelloedd Caerdydd
www.caerdydd.gov.uk/llyfrgelloedd

ACC. No: 02969796

SPECIAL MESSAGE TO READERS

THE ULVERSCROFT FOUNDATION
(registered UK charity number 264873)

was established in 1972 to provide funds for research, diagnosis and treatment of eye diseases. Examples of major projects funded by the Ulverscroft Foundation are:-

- The Children's Eye Unit at Moorfields Eye Hospital, London
- The Ulverscroft Children's Eye Unit at Great Ormond Street Hospital for Sick Children
- Funding research into eye diseases and treatment at the Department of Ophthalmology, University of Leicester
- The Ulverscroft Vision Research Group, Institute of Child Health
- Twin operating theatres at the Western Ophthalmic Hospital, London
- The Chair of Ophthalmology at the Royal Australian College of Ophthalmologists

You can help further the work of the Foundation by making a donation or leaving a legacy. Every contribution is gratefully received. If you would like to help support the Foundation or require further information, please contact:

THE ULVERSCROFT FOUNDATION
The Green, Bradgate Road, Anstey
Leicester LE7 7FU, England
Tel: (0116) 236 4325

website: www.foundation.ulverscroft.com

LEANNA'S MYSTERY TRIP

Three years ago, Leanna and Philip wed after a whirlwind courtship. But married life has fallen short of their dreams. Philip imagines chatting up other women at business conferences, while Leanna wonders whether divorce would be the best way forward. Then, at a dinner party, an argument turns into a challenge when Leanna declares she could slip off somewhere without detection for four months. Is it really possible? And might absence make the heart grow fonder, as she and Philip learn what it's like to live without the other?

Books by Eileen Knowles
in the Linford Romance Library:

THE ASTOR INHERITANCE
MISTRESS AT THE HALL
ALL FOR JOLIE
HOLLY'S DILEMMA
FORGOTTEN BETROTHAL
ROSES FOR ROBINA
THE WYLDES OF CHELLOW HALL

EILEEN KNOWLES

LEANNA'S MYSTERY TRIP

Complete and Unabridged

LINFORD
Leicester

First published in Great Britain in 2018

First Linford Edition
published 2018

Copyright © 2018 by Eileen Knowles
All rights reserved

A catalogue record for this book is available
from the British Library.

ISBN 978–1–4448–3653–0

Published by
F. A. Thorpe (Publishing)
Anstey, Leicestershire

Set by Words & Graphics Ltd.
Anstey, Leicestershire
Printed and bound in Great Britain by
T. J. International Ltd., Padstow, Cornwall

This book is printed on acid-free paper

1

'Are you sure you wouldn't rather go on your own, love?' Leanna said, shaking two paracetamol tablets out of the bottle and swallowing them down with a glass of water. She had worked herself up into a state at the thought of the forthcoming dinner party, so now her head was pounding. All she wanted to do was to lie down quietly and perhaps relax with a good book.

'Don't be silly. Of course I can't go without you. Whatever would they think? Besides, it would spoil the numbers; you know how they like to have everyone paired off. Now, hurry and get yourself dolled up. I don't want us to be the last to arrive.'

Leanna sighed and slowly headed off upstairs. There was little point in arguing, as Philip always got his own way somehow or other; and with the way she was feeling right now, a row was the last thing she needed.

He followed her into the bedroom, still chivvying her. 'What are you thinking of wearing?' he said, seeing the long, floaty dress she had thrown on the bed. Striding over to her wardrobe, he rummaged through the hangers and pulled out a slinky, black, sleeveless number. 'How about this instead?' he said with a smile. 'You always look good in black. Now do get a move on, Leanna; we're going to be late and I hate being the last to arrive.'

Leanna listlessly slipped the dress over her head, thinking it was hardly suitable for the occasion. But what the hell — what did it matter? What did any of it matter? She dabbed on some perfume and located a pair of high-heeled sandals. With a grimace at the dressing-table mirror, she decided to add some dangly earrings and a pearl choker. 'There, that will have to do,' she muttered to herself. Grabbing a beaded clutch bag and a swirling shawl, she marched downstairs.

No matter what she wore, she knew the fashion-conscious Tania, Louisa and Sophie would make her look like a dumpy midget as always. She wondered what Josie Fielding was like. Would she be tall, slim and condescending like the others? she wondered. Oh, why did she feel so inadequate, just because she was small and not exactly slender? She enjoyed cooking, and thought women who prided themselves on living on the odd lettuce leaf just plain stupid.

'Where's the bottle of plonk?' Philip shouted from the living room.

'It's on the dining-room table.'

Philip scurried to collect it, then hustled her impatiently out the door. 'I hope it's got a respectable label, and it's not some of that cheap rubbish from the supermarket.'

Leanna didn't think this worthy of a reply. As they walked briskly along the cul-de-sac and round into the neighbouring crescent, she asked to be reminded of what the Fieldings did for a living.

'I did tell you,' he sighed, irritably. 'Henry's an accountant. The word at the golf club is he's quite a high flyer. Josie, his partner, works as his secretary; and like us, they've no children, so they're just the kind of people we should be cultivating contacts with. He drives a brand new Porsche, and she has a nippy little MX5. I'm dying to see their place. They had it designed to suit their very own specifications, so I guess it's something special. You will try to get involved with the conversation won't you?'

'I hope they're into gardening or cookery then,' Leanna muttered; but fortunately Philip didn't hear, as a beautiful white Mercedes convertible cruised by, distracting him.

'Did you see that?' he said, obviously rattled. 'It was Jerry and Tania. I wonder what that cost?'

'Surely they haven't got in the car just to travel that distance. Why, it can't be more than half a mile. They must want to show it off, I suppose. Is it new, do you reckon?'

'Course it is,' he growled.

Oh dear, she thought, *somebody's nose is going to be put out of joint.* Philip's old-fashioned Jaguar saloon, which he insisted was a quality classic, wouldn't stand a chance, so cars were not for discussion tonight. Well, that suited her. Unlike Philip, to her, cars were just a convenient method of transport. She wasn't interested enough to learn about the different specifications, or worry about the various manufacturers' models. What did it matter what its top speed was or how many miles it did to the litre?

As they approached the exclusive, newly-built bungalow, the front door was flung open wide by a tall, dark-haired man with the physique of a rugby player.

'You must be Leanna,' he said. 'I've been so looking forward to meeting you.' Henry Fielding, their genial host for the evening, ushered them both into the lounge to meet the rest of the guests. 'I think you know everybody. Jerry and Tania over by the window. George and Louisa here, with Damian and Sophie. And this,' he said, putting an arm round a slim blonde, 'is my long-suffering partner, Josie. She's been busy slaving away in the kitchen all day, so I hope you've all got healthy appetites.'

Leanna smiled and accepted the drink she was offered.

'You exaggerate,' Josie giggled, disengaging herself. 'He's miffed because he had to manage the office alone today. But it was only for half a day, darling.'

Pleasant enough, Leanna thought, sinking down onto the nearest settee. The sandals were not as comfortable as she'd been led to believe. How on earth could a few straps cause such a problem? She glanced around at the ultra-modern furnishings, and agreed with Sophie sitting next to her how delightful it all was — but secretly, she thought it dreadful. She guessed it was a designer-this and a designer-that. Not homely. There was nothing even an inch out of place. The best you could say was that it wasn't over-furnished.

She was relieved to see that Josie was not tall and willowy like the other women, but she still had an air of elegance that Leanna could never hope to acquire. She wondered again why Philip had married her. It was on her mind a lot lately. Three years ago she had been an unsophisticated, self-conscious nineteen-year-old feeling a little bereft. Philip's confident manner and pleasure-seeking boyishness bowled her over. Theirs had been a whirlwind courtship and marriage, which she now believed Philip was regretting. He was impetuous by nature, and she suspected her father-in-law had set the ball rolling by mentioning it was time his son got himself a wife, thinking marriage might make him more settled.

Well, it hadn't worked. Philip still acted like an overgrown school kid at times, but now it tended to be overdone and looked ridiculous. She rather liked her in-laws, though. Dennis and Enid were a kind, honest, hardworking couple with down-to-earth values. What a shame Philip didn't take after them.

The meal was truly delightful — light and uncomplicated. Josie was a superb cook, and they didn't stint on the wine either, so the conversation flowed nonstop. Everyone seemed to be enjoying themselves enormously. Jerry had his moment of glory when he gloated about his new set of wheels, and Sophie informed them with smug delight that she was jetting off to the Bahamas the following week to help behind the scenes at a photoshoot. It was all going swimmingly.

'Have you seen there's a new camera monitoring the high street?' George said, casually. 'And they're proposing installing one at the de-restriction signs too. So you'd best watch your step, Jerry. Not sure you know how to keep your thirsty machine below thirty miles an hour.'

'Damned cameras everywhere,' Philip

declared. It was one of his hobby horses. He hated being spied upon, saying his rights were being eroded little by little; but on the other hand, he liked to know what everyone else was doing. Taking a neighbourly interest, he said; but the way he went about it, Leanna thought he was just plain nosey.

'Not long ago you could have driven from John o' Groats to Land's End and not been detected,' Philip continued. 'Now, nobody can move a mile from their own front door without being monitored and checked up on.'

There was general agreement amongst the other guests, and mutterings about what they would like to do if they were in government, when Leanna, the wine having gone to her head, decided that for once she was not going to agree with all her husband decreed. She usually backed him up despite her own personal opinion; but this time, she wasn't going to keep quiet. Why should she?

'I bet I could lose myself,' she said, with quiet determination. 'I could

9

escape detection quite easily. No problem.'

'Never,' Philip said, to the obvious agreement of the others. 'Everywhere you go, you're checked up on. Why, you can't even go out for a meal without leaving a trail via your credit card, and who can manage without one of those these days?'

'I could,' Leanna replied, very calmly, despite Philip glaring at her across the table. She had no relatives who would worry about her; only her husband, who she suspected would be delighted by her absence. 'Quite easily,' she continued, insistently. 'I'll even name the time frame: four months. I'd be back in time for Christmas. Want to bet on it? I'm serious. If I lose, I'll pay £100 to be split between you — and if I win, each of you will have to pay me £100. What do you think of that?'

With much hilarity, they discussed the various problems that would have to be overcome. They all shook their heads in disbelief when Leanna reiterated that she could manage without her credit card and mobile phone. When she had first left school, she had managed to support herself very frugally, and felt that if she had to, she could do so again.

The party broke up shortly afterwards, and Philip was very quiet as they staggered home. He liked to think he was part of the young, swinging scene instead of acting like a competent, twenty-nine-year-old company executive, thought Leanna to herself. Perhaps it was time to put her foot down, consider getting a job and becoming more independent. Possibly even contemplating divorce, considering how out of step with each other they seemed all the time. First, though, she had the challenge to complete.

2

Leanna didn't sleep much that night, despite the alcohol she had consumed, or maybe because of it. She was too excited at the prospect of the next four months. She guessed the others would have forgotten all about the challenge in the morning, and thought it just the wine talking, but she had been serious. She intended going through with it, regardless of the obstacles she would have to overcome. She knew it wouldn't be easy, but she felt confident she could do it; and in any case, it would be fun finding out, and would surely teach Philip the lesson he so badly needed. Why did he have to make such an ass of himself? she wondered. Why couldn't he act more like a grown-up? He held a responsible position — admittedly with the family firm, and not quite as rewarding as Henry's maybe, but still . . .

Some of the difficulties she would have to overcome seemed, at first glance, insurmountable, but they only made Leanna more determined to find an answer. She knew she was feeling cranky. Their marriage had been going through a rough patch, but she knew it wasn't all Philip's fault. She had somehow lost her way — lost her own individuality. She wasn't sure what exactly was wrong, but knew they couldn't carry on as they were. As dawn broke, she listened to a pigeon cooing on the rooftop, and recalled it was Philip who had ended up deliberately goading her into accepting the challenge. Was he trying to tell her something? Did he really feel it was time to put an end to their sham of a marriage? Had he already found someone else?

It was Sunday, and later that day Philip announced he was meeting some chaps for a drink at the golf club, knowing full well Leanna wouldn't join him. She had no interest in golf. Neither did Philip, if the truth was known, but he thought it good for his image to be seen there occasionally, propping up the bar. His golf clubs, though, were still as pristine as the day they were bought. Leanna could tell he was still annoyed at her argumentative attitude at the dinner party, so she spent a pleasant day by herself, pottering in the garden and reflecting on the challenge before her.

*   *   *

After Philip left for work on Monday morning, Leanna made some tea and sat at the kitchen table, prepared to write down her plan of campaign. This was going to be her escape to four months of freedom — with her husband's blessing! What could be better? Perhaps it would make him realise he couldn't have everything his own way all the time, like he seemed to think. She hoped at least that he would miss her, but either way it would be good for both of them to have the time apart — time for reflection. It was a bit of a gamble, she realised, but something she had to do.

She considered waiting until after her birthday, but decided not to. Her in-laws would no doubt be disappointed because they made a big thing of birthdays, but she would make it up to them at Christmas. She recalled her last birthday, when she was twenty-one. Philip's parents had showered her with gifts and organised a wonderful party at their home. She had been made to feel so special when they said they viewed her as the daughter they never had. She hated letting them down, but knew this challenge was something she couldn't put off, or doubts would creep in and put a stop to it.

She began by considering transport and living accommodation. That didn't prove too difficult, as she had already decided to take their old campervan. Recently it had been given a full service, and the tax renewed only the previous week. Philip hadn't wanted to bother, since he never intended using it on the road ever again, but Leanna didn't like the idea of it not being in a useable condition. It had only been used once, to her knowledge — for an expensive, somewhat disastrous trip to the Lake District soon after they met, after which Philip decided he would sell it. He hadn't yet got round to doing so.

Leanna used it as a studio for her art paraphernalia, and as a hideaway where she penned her short stories. Philip told all and sundry she was a writer and artist, which thoroughly embarrassed her, since so far she'd had limited success selling either her stories or her paintings. Writing and painting were her escapes to a fantasy world, away from mundane household chores. Not that she minded doing the housework — in fact, she usually quite enjoyed it — but she still needed something else to occupy her time.

She thought about how to accumulate cash funds so she wouldn't have to use a credit card. £2000 had been agreed as the starting amount — £500 for each month — and the target was to stay undiscovered for four months. She decided to pack the campervan with plenty of tinned food, pasta, and packets of soup. This she didn't think unfair, since most households would have similar stores readily available. She would take her laptop and mobile pay-as-you-go phone for emergencies, but would be untraceable. By the end of the morning she was beginning to feel the plan was coming together nicely, and was quite feasible. She couldn't wait to get started. The sooner the better.

Later that afternoon, she had a surprise visitor — Josie.

'Hi,' she said with a bright smile. 'I was on my way home and thought I'd drop by and give you that recipe that you wanted.'

'How kind. Do come in.'

Leanna wasn't sure what to say to Josie, who was looking extremely elegant in her smart office suit and pristine white blouse.

'I'm in the middle of baking. Do you mind if we talk in the kitchen?' She busied herself with buttering some newly baked scones and organising the cups and saucers, feeling rather awkward. She felt a bit of a fraud being a housewife, since they didn't have children to look after, but in her own way she enjoyed what she did. Should she admit to Josie she was already preparing for her adventure? Should she even remind her of the challenge?

Josie perched casually on a stool at the breakfast bar. 'You're so lucky. I only wish I could stay at home, but unfortunately we have a huge mortgage to pay off. Come to think of it, though, I don't know what I'd do all day if I didn't go to work. It's what I'm used to. Anyway, what I really came round for was to apologise.'

'Oh, why? What for?' Leanna replied, somewhat startled.

Josie sipped her tea before replying. 'It was rather crass of us the other night. I mean, going on about how impossible it would be to disappear, what with family and friends all looking for you. I didn't know. Louisa rang me later and told me about you having lost your family and having nobody now. No relatives, I mean. I am so sorry.'

Leanna sighed with a shrug of her shoulders. 'Don't worry about it. It's something I've got used to. Besides, I have Philip's family now. They've been very good to me.'

'Henry said you were only fifteen when the accident happened. That's so young, to have lost both your parents and your brother. It must have been awful. However did you cope?'

If she thought that was awful, thank goodness she didn't know the rest of the story, thought Leanna. That would really put Josie's sympathy into over-drive. She managed to pass it off with a shrug and quickly changed the subject.

★   ★   ★

For the next couple of days, Leanna went over her scheme looking for snags, and was cautiously optimistic she could pull it off. She didn't tell Philip or any of the others she was seriously contemplating taking them up on the bet. She wanted it to be a complete surprise, to slip away quietly one morning and simply . . . disappear.

She did meet her friend Moira, though, and blurted out to her what she proposed doing, which in hindsight was probably a mistake. She swore Moira to secrecy.

'How on earth will you get away with it?' Moira exclaimed with raised eyebrows. 'Four months is a long time. For a start, you'll need false number plates for the campervan, and a false passport too. How exciting.'

Leanna laughed. 'Oh no, I don't think that'll be necessary. It's not like I'm an escaped convict or anything.'

Moira frowned thoughtfully. 'What if Philip tells the police the campervan's been stolen? And what if you decide to travel to the continent? He may tell the police you're a missing person, so they'll alert customs. I don't think you've thought this through properly.'

'But I've no intention of going abroad, and I'm sure Phil won't inform the police. I'm going to leave him a note so he knows I'll be back in four months, in time for Christmas as agreed. I shan't be far away.'

'Well, don't say I didn't warn you. Hey, I've just had an idea. You know how often people say we could be taken for twins? Well, what if we exchange passports? You take mine just as a precaution, okay? I'm not on the wanted list as far as I know,' she added with a chuckle. 'You'd best let me have yours in case I need to go anywhere, but it's hardly likely as I've no holiday due. It'll be a bit of a lark, and we'll see how vigilant the customs people really are. Oh, I say, this is exciting. I wish I were coming with you.'

Leanna shook her head. 'I have no intention of doing anything so melodramatic or illegal. I just want some time to myself for a while. This was a heaven-sent opportunity.'

Moira grinned. 'Oh well, never mind. I'll just have to keep an eye on Philip for you. But I insist you take my wig. You can wear it with dark glasses and a large floppy hat and pretend you're a famous film star travelling incognito.'

★ ★ ★

It was, in the event, staggeringly easy to slip away. Philip informed her he was going to a conference down in Brighton and would be away for two or three days. That suited Leanna admirably. She would be well hidden before he even knew she had gone. For a brief moment she did wonder whom he would be meeting in Brighton, since he seemed so excited about the trip, but decided not to dwell on that. As far as she knew, he hadn't actually got involved with anyone else since they had been married. It was a sort of game he played, pretending he was a modern-day Casanova; but Leanna felt almost certain that if a woman responded, he would be completely out of his depth and become quite embarrassed. She suspected that for all his show of bravado, he was rather a shy and indecisive individual.

She spent the first morning Philip was away clearing out the campervan of all the miscellaneous junk they had accumulated and giving it a thorough spring clean. Next, she loaded it up with all the things she could think of that she might need for the next four months. She even located the paperwork explaining all about the workings of the campervan, and hoped she would be capable of dealing with it by herself. When they had gone to the Lake District, they'd had to get assistance from fellow campers when it came to connecting it up, and dealing with the water supply and so on. She had felt quite embarrassed, having assumed Philip knew all about such things. She hoped it wouldn't be necessary this time to summon assistance, as she wanted to be as self-sufficient as possible so as not to draw attention to herself.

When it was time to go, Leanna felt extremely nervous, and almost sick with excitement. She knew it would look as if she had taken leave of her senses, and yet in her heart she felt it was the right thing to do — for both their sakes. The campervan had been parked behind the garage, some distance from the road, and it would be the first time she had ever driven it. She had passed her test, so she sometimes drove the Jaguar — mainly when Philip had been drinking — but the campervan was so much bigger. Dauntingly so. The man from the garage had taken it away for its MOT and parked it back neatly against the garage wall, but otherwise Philip was the only one who drove it.

Taking a deep breath, Leanna switched it on, and it immediately sprang to life as if eager to be on the road. She smoothly engaged first gear and inched it carefully forward, stalling twice before she got the measure of the clutch. She listened for scraping sounds; but apart from driving over the edge of the lawn and grazing the conifer hedge, she managed to manoeuvre onto the road without serious mishap. With a huge sigh of relief, she set off on her journey.

Soon the narrow, cluttered roads of their neighbourhood were left behind and Leanna was out on the open road heading for the coast. It was good to be free and unconstrained, with nobody criticising when she dawdled and missed an overtaking opportunity or bounced in potholes through not paying attention. She was so happy that she switched on the radio. She found a channel with popular music suiting her mood and laughed at how carefree she felt.

She very soon got acclimatised to the size of the van, and in some ways found it easier to drive than the Jaguar, especially since she didn't have Philip fussily issuing her with frequent and unnecessary instructions. It was only a small two-berth affair, complete with mini-bathroom. It also housed a small fridge and a microwave. What more could she need? Using her mobile, she had already booked into a small campsite on the outskirts of Whitby for a few days. She had chosen the site at random, happy in the knowledge that even though it wasn't far away, Philip would never have heard of it, so she should be safe there for the time being.

York was soon left behind, and by the time she reached Malton and the turnoff for Pickering, she was feeling confident about her ability to cope with driving the campervan. That was a load off her mind, since she didn't know yet how much travelling she would have to do in the next four months. She was going to play it by ear. £500 a month wouldn't go far, so she wouldn't want to spend too much on fuel. Apart from paying for the campsite, the only other expense would be for food — unless she could forage the hedgerows and live for free. That made her chuckle. Perhaps living frugally, she would actually lose some of this weight she seemed to be gaining.

As she approached the top of the infamous Saltersgate Bank, she was ready for morning coffee, so she pulled into the large car park and switched off with a sigh of pleasure. She had truly escaped and only hoped Philip wouldn't be too annoyed or upset when he found out. She hoped he would understand and appreciate why she was doing this — for both their benefits.

Before her was the glorious panoramic view of the heather-clad North York Moors bathed in misty sunshine. While she drank her coffee, she glanced at the map and knew the next stretch of road was the one she most feared, so she got out to stretch her legs. The valley below was quite spectacular, and obviously a target for walkers. She watched as a group of ramblers strapped rucksacks to their backs and strode off down the slope, chatting companionably. She was about to get back in the campervan when she spotted a steam train edging its way along the valley bottom. It looked wonderful, and gave her the sensation of having stepped back in time. Maybe she would have the opportunity to take a ride on it if it wasn't too expensive.

Five minutes later she cautiously set off down the steep hill with its tight hairpin bend, and having negotiated it with no trouble, headed for the notorious Blue Bank above the village of Sleights a few miles away, feeling slightly reassured. As she approached Blue Bank, she caught up with a lorry, and thought it best to remain behind it. The lorry looked substantial. It ran through her mind that if the brakes of the campervan failed, she could rely on the lorry to stop her. Philip would have a fit if he knew what she was thinking, she realised with wry grin. He would have needed to overtake the lorry so as not to be held up.

She arrived in the village quite safely, and parted company with the lorry at the bridge over the river where she was to turn right. This was another tricky bit, as she knew the campsite wasn't far away, and she didn't want to pass it and have to do any reversing, which was one skill she never felt comfortable with.

Ten minutes later, she arrived. Eskside campsite looked absolutely delightful. The grounds were well kept and attractively laid out, and it was only a small place with perhaps fifteen or twenty caravans. It was close to the river and in walking distance of Whitby. It couldn't be more perfect from her point of view.

Joe Jessop, the campsite owner, directed her onto the appropriate site and even helped her get set up, for which she was extremely grateful. She thought she could possibly have managed by herself, but it would have taken her a lot longer and she was more than ready for something to eat. Unfortunately, a blanket of fog crept up the river while she was preparing some sandwiches, so she settled down to read the brochures Joe had given her about what to see and do in the surrounding area. It all sounded fabulous and she smiled contentedly.

She had visited Whitby once before with Philip, who stated it was the last time he would be coming since it was impossible to park, the streets were far too narrow, and there were too many tourists wandering about willy-nilly. What little Leanna had seen of it, though, she had found appealing, and she was looking forward to exploring. She thought it felt homely. For the moment, though, she settled in and started her diary, which she intended filling in daily to record her four-month exile. Momentarily she did consider phoning her in-laws, but thought there was the possibility her phone would give away her location; and so she decided, regretfully, to abandon the idea.

3

Philip headed for Brighton, anticipating an enjoyable few days away on his own. He was glad Leanna had turned down his suggestion that she accompany him. It had been a mere courtesy to ask her, knowing full well she was hardly likely to join him. It wasn't that he didn't like being married, but there were times when he wanted to escape and feel totally liberated. He supposed he was still niggled by Leanna's recent behaviour. Take for instance the scene she'd made at the dinner party the other night. What had possessed her to deliberately oppose everyone with her outrageous comments? Why couldn't she have stayed quiet like she usually did? It was one thing to cause an argument at home over some trifling matter, but to show them both up in public was going too far. He wasn't sure what to do about it, and perhaps the weekend conference would help give him time to think.

He wondered who would be at the conference. He recalled a pleasant blonde he'd met the previous year. She had definitely given him the eye. The thought of some guaranteed flirting made him smile as he finally gunned the Jaguar past a slow-moving, irritating Mini he'd been following for ages. Yes, this weekend conference had come up at just the right moment. He knew his father wasn't too pleased at him going, saying it would be a complete waste of time; but it wasn't for the business side of things he wanted to go. He enjoyed meeting the exciting, trendy people who gravitated to such gatherings. What the eye doesn't see, the heart doesn't grieve over, was his motto.

⋆   ⋆   ⋆

Three days later, he arrived home feeling tired, disgruntled and decidedly out of sorts. The conference had in no way lived up to his expectations. The new venue was drab and the seminars exceedingly dull, the food had been appalling — and to crown it all, the delegates were all depressingly old and staid. To make matters worse, the weather had turned wet and the car had started playing up. To say he wasn't in the best frame of mind was putting it mildly. He parked the car on the drive, hardly registering the house was in darkness. Finding the front door locked, he fumbled for his keys, cursing crossly.

'Hi, I'm back,' he shouted, switching on the hall lights once he got inside. No response. Dropping his overnight bag with a loud clatter, Philip marched up the stairs, fully expecting Leanna to be fast asleep, despite explicitly telling her he would be returning that evening. Surely the least he could expect was a welcome home kiss and a light snack. She knew he would be hungry because he hated motorway service station food.

He had driven nonstop and was weary and starving.

He burst into the bedroom and switched on the light, only to find the bed unoccupied. He stared in disbelief — no Leanna? Where on earth was she? It was late. Normally she didn't like being out after dark, alone. He went back down the stairs two at a time, and after investigating the lounge, went into the kitchen, feeling completely mystified and not liking the empty feel. She was always there waiting for him whenever he returned home. Where could she have got to? He hoped she was all right. Had she taken the hump because he hadn't rung? Had he forgotten some anniversary?

He was filling the kettle when he spied her note, propped up against the teapot. Quickly skimming through its contents, he couldn't believe what he was reading. She had actually taken the challenge seriously. She'd gone and left him — for *four whole months*. He slumped down and held his head in his hands. What had he done to deserve this? He would never live it down. The challenge had been a joke, for goodness' sake.

★   ★   ★

Philip spent an uncomfortable few days coming to terms with Leanna's desertion. He hadn't yet told anyone she was missing, but knew he would have to before long. The trouble was, he didn't know what to say. *My wife has taken it upon herself to abandon me. She's gone off in the campervan, saying she will be back in four months' time to claim the reward.* What on earth would people think, for God's sake? He knew he would at least have to tell his parents. They were always asking after her, and he knew his mother often popped in to see her. He half-suspected his mother thought more of Leanna than of her own son.

After a week of burnt offerings or mediocre meals consumed at the local pub, he was starting to fully appreciate how much Leanna did for him. He had never had to cook a meal or wash and iron a shirt in his life. First, his mother had done everything for him; and when he had married, he'd expected his wife to take over such chores. He couldn't be bothered to learn about using the microwave, or defrosting food from the freezer. With no clean clothes to wear, and having scorched his best shirt in an attempt at ironing, he finally accepted he would have to explain the silly challenge to his parents, and see if his mother would at least do his washing.

'Philip,' his mother said, somewhat irritably, when she heard his sorry tale of woe, 'it's time you pulled yourself together. Leanna is a wonderful woman, and to be quite frank, better than you deserve. If you're not careful, she'll leave you for good, and I for one wouldn't blame her, the way you treat her. She would never have accepted such a silly challenge if you'd only seen how unhappy she's been of late.'

Philip frowned. Had he been so

obtuse? Had she really been unhappy? She didn't often say much, and seemed content with her own company. She was a capable housewife with hobbies such as her writing. What else did she want?

'Of course I'll do your washing, and keep an eye on the house, Philip. More for Leanna's sake than yours, though; I wouldn't want her returning to find the place a tip. But for goodness' sake stop behaving like a stupid adolescent. Marriage is a serious commitment. You do love Leanna, don't you?'

'Of course I do, Mum. I just don't know what she wants.'

'Well, you'd best find out then, hadn't you? Or I'm telling you, my lad, you'll lose her. She may be young, but she's got a good head on her shoulders. She won't have taken off lightly, I'll be bound. Something must have upset her.'

Philip didn't ever take kindly to being lectured, but did take his mother's advice seriously. He knew he didn't want to go back to being single again. He liked being married, and he loved Leanna. He just couldn't understand what he'd been doing wrong to cause her to be miserable. They had a nice home in a lovely area. They had a good living standard, holidays, lots of friends. What more did she want?

One thing he decided he could do right away was to spend more time with the business. It was something that would please his parents, at any rate. Recently he knew he hadn't been overexerting himself in that department, and his father was always on about his lax timekeeping. It would show Leanna he was taking life seriously, wouldn't it? Was that what she wanted?

When he got home each evening, he wandered round the empty house, missing Leanna more than he could ever have believed. He couldn't get interested in television, or reading books or newspapers. He didn't want to visit the pub too often for fear of bumping into his friends. He knew Leanna didn't really care for them — and, if truth be known, he wondered if he did either. He thought about what they would say when they heard Leanna had accepted the challenge. To them, he imagined, it would be one huge joke. He guessed their responses would be something like:

Good show, old man.

I wish my wife would take off for a while, and then I could see more of my secretary.

Why didn't we think of sending all the wives off and become bachelors again?

There would be loud guffaws, and he didn't think he could bear it. All pretty distasteful, when you thought about it.

One night, though, he dropped in early at the local for a bite to eat. He couldn't face the desolate house without a stiff drink inside him. He settled himself in a corner and studied the menu, hoping it was too early for any of his friends to be about. He placed his order and sat brooding about life in general, trying to recall the happy times not all that long ago. When he first met Leanna they had spent some lovely weekends getting out and about, but he couldn't recall what they had actually done. Where had he gone wrong?

He thought about their friends, Henry, Damian, Jerry, George, and their wives. These were people they had met since they got married and come to live in the area. They were all young, upwardly mobile couples like themselves, keen to enjoy the good life while they could. He had thought Leanna liked meeting people and arranging dinner parties. She always did it so competently, and appeared unflustered; but maybe he was mistaken. After all, she was a good deal younger than the others. Perhaps also it was because she had no relatives of her own. He could understand that. He wouldn't like not to have any family, even if they did give him a hard time occasionally.

Leanna's friend Moira arrived in the pub. She must have come straight from work as she was wearing her tight, grey, office suit. Seeing Philip, she made a beeline for him. Without a by-your-leave, she plonked herself down opposite and asked how he was. She appeared to know Leanna had left — goodness knew how — and seemed intent on accompanying him at the table. She asked what he had ordered, and said she would have the same.

'I'll do all I can to help,' she said, reaching over to squeeze his hand. 'Four months is a long time to be on your own.'

'Oh, I can manage, thanks. I'm not exactly helpless,' Philip said, leaning away from her. He never felt very comfortable in Moira's company. She was a bit overwhelming. Although she resembled Leanna outwardly, enough for people to remark on it, she hadn't Leanna's gentleness.

Moira leaned forward. 'No, of course not. But there are some things that need a woman's touch, aren't there?' She winked and patted her hair. 'All I'm saying is, if there's anything I can do to make life bearable while Leanna's away, you only have to ask. Have you heard from her, by the way? Is she all right? Know where she's gone? I must say, I was stunned when she told me about the whole idea.'

Philip had a horrible suspicion he had just been propositioned, and was glad when the food arrived. He hoped it would put an end to her chatter. Unfortunately, Moira had a talent for eating and talking at the same time. He decided he would prefer beans on toast at home rather than go through this again. How had he ever thought Moira was like Leanna? In looks maybe, but there the similarity ended.

*   *   *

Philip was working late at the office on the last day of August. He had nothing to hurry home for, and he wanted to complete the end-of-month accounts. For once he was being diligent, and was on top of things office-wise. He was buckling down to some hard graft to show his father how capable he was. For some reason, he didn't find it to be the chore he had expected. He rather liked the feeling of achievement. Before, he had merely completed whatever tasks his father asked of him, and little else. Even those had been done half-heartedly. Now, having taken his mother's lecture to heart, he started looking at ways of improving the firm, and taking a real interest.

The phone rang; he nearly didn't answer it since it was after office hours, and more than likely a wrong number. They'd had a few of those recently. Eventually, when it continued to ring, he grabbed it irritably.

'Thank goodness I've found you, Philip.' It was his mother, sounding terribly upset. 'It's your father. He's had a mild stroke. Can you come?'

Philip was horrified. 'Of course, Mum. I'll be right with you.'

He hurriedly closed down the computer and left, feeling panicky. How serious was a mild stroke? Didn't it affect a person's speech? He thought there could be some numbness too. How long would his father be out of action? Would he be able to cope with running the business? All sorts of thoughts ran through his head as he quickly drove the short distance to the family home. He didn't like the sound of it. His father had always been in such good health. He was never poorly. Philip couldn't recall the last day off he'd had, and he rarely took a holiday.

His mother looked tearful and hugged him. 'The doctor's been, and wanted him to go into hospital for tests. But you know your father — he's adamant he's not going.'

'How serious is it, Mum?'

'It was only a very minor stroke apparently, nothing too serious; but he's lost some use of his left side, and seems to have a balance problem. I understand the best we can do is keep him in bed and make sure he's not worrying about the office. I've already rung my friend who's a nurse, and she's promised to look in every day. I shouldn't have rung you, only I was that worried . . . '

'You did the right thing, Mum. I'll go and reassure Dad. All that really matters is for him to get better, and I'll do what I can to keep the business up and running, so he's not to worry. After all, it'll be my responsibility eventually, though I didn't think it would come about quite like this. It's time he was thinking about semi-retirement, isn't it?' he said with a gentle smile. 'Time he took you on that world cruise you're always on about.'

His mother smiled through her tears. 'Oh, those were just pipe dreams. You know I'd never get your dad on a boat. Now then, will you stay the night, love? I've made up the bed in your old room just in case.'

'Yes, of course I will. Any chance of a snack? I'm starving.' He could see how distressed his mother was, and thought it might help to give her something ordinary and mundane to concentrate on.

After he had been in to see his father, he wandered into the kitchen and sat down at the breakfast bar. 'How are you, Mum? Really? Are you all right?' The thought struck him that he had taken his parents for granted — expected them always to be there. He'd forgotten how old they were. Lots of people retired at fifty-five these days, and his dad was nearer sixty. He didn't know what he would do without them. It seemed as if things were piling up on him, and he was beginning to feel overwhelmed. He wished Leanna was here. She would know what to do, what to say, despite being so much younger. It wasn't that he was unsympathetic; he just didn't know what was expected of him.

His mother nodded and placed a cheese omelette in front of him. 'Tea, or something stronger?' she asked while buttering some bread.

'Tea's fine.'

His mother sat opposite him and

poured the tea. She seemed calmer now. 'Have you made contact with Leanna? It's her birthday tomorrow,' she reminded him.

'No, I haven't. I've kept trying, but I don't think she wants to hear from me.'

'What did you get her for a present?'

'I haven't — not yet,' he admitted, shame-faced. 'What do you suggest?'

His mother patted his hand. 'That's something you'll have to decide. You've got plenty of time before she returns. I'm sure there's something you know she wants if you put your mind to it.'

'She wouldn't really leave me, would she?'

'Who knows? She's young and has had a lot to contend with over the years, so it's up to you to be more grounded, and help her. She's a lovely lass and does try so hard to please everyone.'

Philip nodded. 'Yes, I guess you're right. I'll make it up to her when she gets back,' he added with a frown.

4

Once darkness fell, Leanna felt nervous and not a little scared. The situation was not helped by the heated arguments between rowdy, bottle-throwing youths close by. She realised how isolated and vulnerable she was, and wondered if it was a mistake being here alone. What would happen if someone broke into the van? What if they set fire to it? What if . . .

The next morning she took herself to task. She only had to ring Joe Jessop and it would be for him to sort things out. There really was nothing for her to be afraid of. All the same, she decided she would buy herself a personal alarm when she went into Whitby. She would have liked to have a dog for company — she'd often said it — but knew that was something she would have to talk to Philip seriously about. You couldn't just get a dog short-term to suit yourself.

A few days later, Leanna went along to see Joe to ask about staying longer — possibly the whole four months — but was disappointed to learn he couldn't accommodate her at the campsite.

'Oh dear,' she said. 'I guess it's still school holidays. Unfortunately, this was a spur-of-the-moment decision of mine, and I was so looking forward to staying at least several more weeks. I'm writing a novel, and this is such a wonderful, peaceful place. It's ideal. I don't suppose you can suggest anywhere else in this area I could try?'

He frowned thoughtfully and shook his head. 'I'm almost fully booked for the next few weeks, like most folk around here. I had a last-minute cancellation, which was why it was free this last week. I really don't know of anywhere with vacancies. Like you say, it's school holidays. Everywhere is full.' Seeing her disappointment, he went on, 'But I do have an alternative suggestion. If you don't mind being off site and closer to the farmhouse, I could fix you up with a power supply from yon barn. It might be a bit primitive, so there'd be a reduction in the cost naturally. The facilities being somewhat more limited, you understand.'

'Oh, that would be great.' She jumped at the offer, especially as it would cost less.

'You'd have further to go to the showers and the amenity block, and the farmyard does get a bit messy after heavy rain.' He looked up at the clear blue sky. 'Fortunately I don't have cows anymore, so it's not quite as bad as it used to be.'

Leanna laughed. 'I don't mind at all, and fortunately I remembered to pack my wellies.' She was happy to accept any suggestion so long as she didn't have to move far. She wasn't looking for perfection, just a simple place to stay that didn't cost a lot. There was always the chance if she did move she may be spotted by one of Philip's friends. She had thought to travel to Scotland, but didn't want to spend the money and wouldn't know where to go anyway.

All in all, the new site suited Leanna very well. She was now remote from the rest of the campers, and the van was not visible from the road either — not that she expected Philip would find her there even if he was out looking. The thought nagged at her that perhaps he wouldn't bother doing anything about seeking her out. Perhaps he even hoped she would never return. What would he tell the neighbours? How would he explain her absence to his parents? She wished she could ring them to explain, but she knew she couldn't because her behaviour was a puzzle even to herself.

Life in the campervan felt very strange to begin with, and a little claustrophobic. After looking after their three-bedroom house, the simple chores were a doddle. So much so, Leanna had too much spare time. She had soon read all the books she had brought with her, and began scouring the charity shops for cheap paperbacks. Whitby had a fair selection, and she chuckled to herself when she thought of what Philip would say at the very idea of her entering such a shop. *But other people have owned them.* She could almost hear the horror in his voice. *You don't know where they've been.*

The countryside noises could also be quite alarming, she found, especially at night, but being so close to the farmhouse she felt reasonably safe. For several days she didn't stir far from the farm, but eventually she became more interested in the locality in which she had elected to spend time. She had been there two weeks and begun crossing off the days on a calendar she had pinned up on the wall.

Leanna had deliberately not switched on her phone so as not to be cowed by any messages from Philip, demanding to know where she was and possibly coercing her into returning. She could imagine his frustration and anger when he returned from his trip to find her note, and wondered how he would cope on the domestic front, as he had hardly lifted a finger in the house in all the time they'd been married — or outside it, for that matter. Her mother-in-law was a keen gardener and had taken her under her wing, showing her how to manage the weedy plot they had inherited. Leanna had taken to it with a passion, and now thoroughly enjoyed being outside taking care of the shrubs and flowerbeds. She only hoped things wouldn't deteriorate too much while she was away.

The housework was something else. Would Philip call in someone to assist? Moira, perhaps? The only time she recalled Philip cooking anything was when she went down with flu and spent a few days in bed. He thought he had been so clever opening a tin of soup and warming it up for her, but then disappeared to the pub for his own lunch.

Once she got used to being alone, Leanna enjoyed the freedom and solitude. It was bliss lying in bed for as long as she wanted, and getting a meal or snack to please herself. She could go for long walks, or sit reading; whatever took her fancy, with nobody to countermand her. She had no one chuntering at her to do this or do that. No providing fancy gourmet meals. It was brilliant.

After a while, though, she began to feel guilty. Ever since she lost her family, she'd had to get used to being self-sufficient, but she wondered how Philip was managing with nobody to look after him. She wouldn't be surprised to find out that was why he'd married her in the first place. He had needed a willing slave and she had been elected. There had been other reasons too, of course, and he had been very supportive about her writing. Should she ring to let him know she was all right? She needn't say where she was staying. But no; she decided she would wait a little while longer before switching on her mobile.

* * *

The first of September arrived. Her birthday. Leanna tried ringing Philip, hoping for a reassuring chat, but was terribly disappointed when there was no reply. The answering machine had been switched off, so she couldn't even leave a message. Feeling hurt and not a little put out, she went for a long walk along the sands. Surely he would expect to hear from her on her birthday? *Right*, she thought, *if that's how he wants to play it*. She would leave her mobile switched off in future. She could cope perfectly well on her own.

By the time she reached Sandsend, she was feeling peckish, so decided to indulge herself with a meal at a small riverside restaurant. Normally she hated eating alone in such places, but the thought of a celebratory meal back at the campervan of mushroom omelette or tuna pasta held little appeal. If she were back home, she would probably be having a pleasant meal out with Philip and his parents. By now, Dennis and Enid would know about the challenge, and she wondered what they thought. Would they feel she had let them down because she hadn't been round to see them before she left? She hoped not. She wondered what Philip had told them and hoped they would understand.

She located a corner table and sat with her back to the other diners, trying to imagine they didn't exist. She took out a paperback and pretended to read, but all the time was wondering what Philip was doing. Was he out on the town enjoying himself with some woman for company? With that thought in mind, she ordered a glass of white wine and the house speciality. She had long since got used to being a lonely individual, but all the same it would have been nice if . . .

Her thoughts returned to Philip, and she wondered if they would be together for her next birthday. She toyed with the freshly caught fish on her plate, feeling depressed. She'd had such hopes for her marriage, wanting a home and family. She'd had visions when they were first married of a gaggle of children and animals romping round their contented, happy home. She couldn't recall having discussed it with Philip; she had just assumed he would want a family. But Philip made a point of making friends with child-free couples and seemed awkward with the few children he came in contact with.

Giving the dessert trolley a miss, Leanna paid the bill and wandered back along the seashore, a bit down in the dumps. The food had been mediocre. The sauce was too bland in her opinion, and the vegetables over-cooked, so she regretted having spent the money. It certainly hadn't cheered her up.

That night, relenting a little, she tried once more to ring Philip. She waited until late, having given him time to return from the office, perhaps having stopped for a snack on the way home. Would it please him to hear from her? She found that she was looking forward to hearing his voice. But again, the phone rang and rang, and in the end she had to give up. She switched off her mobile, feeling miserable, deserted and depressed.

* * *

Another week went by, and Leanna had at last made a start on the novel she had talked about writing for more years than she cared to remember. It was going to be based on her life so far, but made into a fiction, or even romantic love story; she wasn't quite sure how it would turn out yet. At least it gave her something to do and helped to pass the time as she reflected on the ifs and buts of her life so far. Somehow the days appeared considerably longer than they'd been at home, perhaps because she didn't have a television with endless soaps to distract her. She had a small radio and CD player to keep her company; but while the weather was fine, she thought she should get out in the fresh air as much as possible.

Her funds were doing nicely, as she was living economically. What with the walking and the simple meals, she was feeling much fitter and healthier than ever before. Joe was a darling, often leaving her a present of a few eggs or fresh vegetables, which were very welcome. Leanna repaid him with the odd bottle of wine once she learned he enjoyed a drop of burgundy of an evening. Occasionally, she missed dressing up and going out for a slap-up meal, or having conversations with the neighbours. She missed the garden too, and hoped Philip was at least keeping the lawn cut and free of leaves. She very much doubted if he would do the necessary tree pruning, or clear the greenhouse and wash down the staging. That would all have to be left until next year now.

She lived in jeans, T-shirts and thick woollies now the weather had turned colder, and kept her distance from the other campers for fear of being recognised. She had taken to wearing her hair scrunched up under a hat when she went out, to cover up her attention-grabbing auburn hair. Other times she donned the wig Moira had lent her, but she wasn't too keen on it and wished she'd got a blonde one instead. Philip would have a fit if he saw her, but she didn't care.

September seemed to pass very quickly. It had been a lovely month weather-wise, and she had even developed a nice tan that made her look and feel healthy. She was beginning to think Philip wasn't even looking for her. Perhaps, as she had thought initially, he was taking the time out to review whether he wished to remain married. She'd like to think they could work out their differences and have a happy marriage, but only time would tell.

5

Philip was relieved his father was improving so quickly. It had been only a very minor stroke, but it was a wake-up call for all of them. Philip found coping at the office on his own a terrible strain, but was determined his father would see he was capable and could be relied upon. That was his top priority, since Leanna seemed to be unreachable. He spent most of the week at the office or with his parents, but at the weekend returned home. He felt his mother was now coping fine, and he needed time alone with his thoughts in his own home. Unfortunately, home didn't seem so homely and welcoming without Leanna.

That night he sat by the fire feeling lonely and depressed. He thought about Leanna, wondering what she normally did all day while he was at work. Maybe she should get a part-time job after all. He hadn't thought it necessary before, since they didn't need the money — but he began to see that maybe it wasn't about whether or not they needed the money. Should they move house? Perhaps she wasn't happy with the area they lived in, although she'd never said so. She always appeared content, and proud of the garden in particular. When she returned, they would have to spend more time talking, discussing what they both wanted — have a good old heart to heart. He did so hope she was all right. He missed her so. He only wished she would turn on her damned mobile phone.

Philip spent the Saturday tidying up the garden, and had a huge bonfire. He smiled to himself, thinking his mother would be proud to see him knuckling down to such grubby work. He ran the vacuum cleaner round the house, and went shopping at the supermarket — all chores he would never usually have contemplated. Shopping was quite an eye-opener. He had no idea what to buy or where anything was, but he found the frozen food department fascinating. He began to prepare a few edible meals, although he knew he would never be a gourmet cook and couldn't compete with what Leanna prepared. He was continually surprising himself with what he could achieve, and found pleasure in attaining each small milestone, but all the time wishing Leanna was there to share it with him.

He found it surprising how many little things he missed. She was good at running their home, and never seemed to run out of vital items such as toothpaste, like he did. She knew how to cope with the temperamental washing machine, and could produce a meal in minutes. He missed her company when they watched the television; even the comedy programmes didn't seem funny without her chuckling beside him. Oh, how he missed her.

★ ★ ★

On Sunday, he made the big decision to sell his beloved Jaguar. He knew it wasn't a sensible car for him to use, since it was somewhat unpredictable at the best of times and not exactly practical. Leanna found it difficult to drive, having passed her test in a small runabout, so she would no doubt be pleased if he traded it in for something smaller and younger. He had bought the Jaguar as a sort of status symbol, but the upkeep was horrendously expensive, quite apart from it being tricky to start on damp, misty mornings. Before his father's illness, it hadn't mattered if he was late in to work, but now he needed more reliability.

What should he choose? He spent the day browsing car magazines and the internet. By early evening he had placed an advert in the 'for sale' section of the classic car site. By the time Leanna returned, she would find whole a lot of things would be different, he thought.

In no time at all, Philip sold his Jaguar and purchased a medium-sized

Mercedes saloon. He felt saddened to see his old car disappear, but knew it was the right thing to do. The new car had many refinements, and he took pleasure in seeing the personalised number plate he'd bought too. It had been a bit of an extravagance, but he felt he needed a little perk.

The next weekend he drove to the golf club. He only meant to drop in for a drink and chat with Henry, thinking that perhaps now he was taking more of an interest in the business, he would have things in common with him. While he was propping up the bar, a middle-aged man approached, asking Philip if he would care for a round of golf. He said he was a newcomer and would welcome someone showing him the ropes.

'Sorry, but . . . Well, I'm a bit rusty,' Philip said, trying to recall when he'd last had a round. 'My clubs haven't seen the light of day for several weeks,' he added with a wry grin.

'No problem,' the chap replied. 'I'm

not much of a golfer either. I'm really only here for the exercise. The name's Jack.'

'Philip,' he responded with a smile, wondering what he'd let himself in for.

As they walked out to the first tee, Jack said he had recently moved to the area, and his wife thought golf would be a good way for him to meet people.

'Does she play?' Philip asked.

'Goodness, no. She just wants me out from under her feet.'

Philip chuckled. 'My wife's not interested either. Maybe the two should get together.'

They enjoyed the game, although other serious club members wouldn't have approved of some of the strokes; and Philip was glad he hadn't backed down like he'd been going to. They had been pretty evenly matched all the way round, though at the last hole by some stroke of luck Philip managed to win. It cheered him up no end. When they were once again propping up the bar, Jack asked what Philip did for a living.

'Oh, it's a family concern. Office equipment. We have a shop in the city centre, and a warehouse on the industrial estate. I spend most of my time at the latter.'

'Interesting. You may be just the person I've been looking for. I may be able to put some business your way.'

Before Philip could reply, Henry Fielding barged in, slapping him on the back. 'Long time, no see, Phil. How is that gorgeous wife of yours? Not seen her around lately.'

Philip was distinctly annoyed. Jack was about to put business his way. It would be new business and very welcome. He turned to introduce Jack to Henry.

'We've already met,' Jack said rather tersely, and quickly swallowed his drink. 'Thanks for the game, Philip. Nice to have you met you, but I must be going now. Mustn't be late for lunch. See you around.'

Henry placed his order with the barman and motioned Philip to a table in the corner. 'Sorry if that appeared a bit rude, but I thought you ought to know — I wouldn't put too much faith in that chap. He's been hanging about here a lot recently, and always makes sure the other player wins.'

'Is that a problem?' Philip asked, still slightly rattled.

Henry rubbed his hands together. 'It gets you in the right frame of mind to be talked into one of his little schemes. I overheard another member say he thought he'd been duped out of a rather large sum of money. I don't know the ins and outs of it, but so far, I gather he hasn't received the goods. All I'm saying is, be wary. That's all.'

'Thanks for the warning,' Philip said stiffly.

'Well, you're my mate, and that's what mates do, isn't it? By the way, we haven't had a get-together for quite a while. Josie was only saying the other night that we ought to do it again soon. I think she wants to swap recipes with your wife or something. How about it?'

Philip shrugged his shoulders. 'Sure, sounds good to me, but I'm afraid Leanna's away at the moment.' He was going to leave it at that, but then decided to come clean. He took a swig of his drink and smiled broadly. 'You may recall the challenge, the one we made at your last dinner party? Well, Leanna took it seriously. She's gone away for four months as agreed, so isn't expected back until Christmas.'

Henry looked incredulous. 'Good heavens! I can't believe it. Well, I never. That takes some guts, I can tell you. I can't imagine doing anything like that. Have you no idea where she is then?'

'No, I'm afraid not,' Philip replied, shaking his head and sighing. 'She could be anywhere. She went off in our old campervan and just disappeared. She's not answering her mobile, and her credit card hasn't been used either. I just don't know . . . She went while I was at a conference in Brighton, and left a note saying she'd be back to claim the reward. £100 from each of you, wasn't it? You'd better start saving your pennies.'

Henry chuckled. 'She'll jolly well deserve it if she lasts that long. Have you tried finding her?'

'Not really. I've been rather busy with work, because my dad's been ill. I thought I'd tootle round the area at the weekend, but she could be just about anywhere. I don't know where to start looking.'

Henry took a swig of his pint. 'Well, I hope she's all right, that's all I can say. The weather could turn nasty, and it will be a mite cold in a camper, won't it? Perhaps we should have a get-together and decide what to do? I'll contact the others and arrange something. Could be quite fun — a treasure-hunt kind of thing.'

★   ★   ★

Philip was surprised by the others' reactions when the five men met the next weekend. Henry had obviously

70

filled them in, and they all seemed keen to find Leanna.

'What's your best guess where she'd go, Phil?' Henry asked when they were all seated in a corner alcove of the Red Lion with their pints of locally brewed ale.

Philip shrugged his shoulders. 'I really have no idea. As you know, she has no relatives, and she's not shown any interest in anywhere specifically. We went to the Lake District once, and she seemed to like that area, but I think she'd find the hills a bit daunting in the campervan.'

'If she's taken the camper, she'll have to stay on a site somewhere,' Damian mused. 'She can't wild-camp for long, you know.'

'I don't think she'd wild-camp at all,' Philip said. 'She doesn't like being out after dark. Besides, she'd need all the facilities of a campsite. I don't honestly think she'd travel far afield. She's not keen on motoring, and she's never driven the campervan before now. I think she might be finding it a bit of a handful.'

'Okay, so how about if we split up the typical areas and each take one?' suggested George. 'I, for one, will take the Peak District. I'll check as many of the campsites as I can find. Louisa likes pottering round Buxton and Bakewell, so that won't be any hardship.'

'I'll take the Lake District,' replied Henry promptly. 'Josie and I were thinking of popping over there for the weekend soon anyway.'

'I don't suppose she'll want to go abroad, will she?' Jerry asked. 'I was just thinking, Hull isn't that far away; she could've got a ferry.'

Philip shook his head. 'I very much doubt it, although her passport is missing.'

'Tania and I will look around the Dales, then,' Jerry said.

'What does that leave Phil and me?' asked Damian.

'The North Yorkshire Moors perhaps, and the Wolds,' Jerry answered. 'There are plenty of campsites along the coast, don't forget.'

'All right, I suppose I'd better take the Wolds,' said Damian. 'The wife has a relative who runs a B&B at Filey. She's always nagging me to take her there.'

'That leaves the wild Yorkshire Moors for you then, Phil,' said Jerry.

'How exactly are we going to go about this?' Philip asked. 'I don't know about you lot, but I'm pretty well tied up with work at the moment. There's only Sunday, as far as I'm concerned, and I'm not sure what I can do in one day.'

'We're all busy, but don't forget the financial implications,' said Jerry.

'Exactly,' replied Henry. '£100 each is a lot of beer money.'

6

October arrived — wet, windy and much, much colder than the previous month. Leanna's novel progressed in leaps and bounds. She was optimistically hoping to have the first draft completed by Christmas, having set herself that as a target. On the whole she was inclined to look on the bright side of things and make the best of situations, but just occasionally a feeling of sadness tended to overwhelm her. When that happened, she pulled on her trainers and set off for a brisk walk along the seashore, often to Sandsend and back. She found walking along the sands and cliff-tops therapeutic, remembering all the things she used to like before she met Philip; simple things like walking in the rain and listening to classical music.

She enjoyed a quiet drink in a cosy old-world pub — not one of the trendy new gin palaces he preferred. In short, she had found herself again, and liked what she'd found. She was in no hurry to return to the life she'd been living; and yet in a way she did still love Philip. She loved the Philip she thought she had married — not the pig-headed, opinionated person he'd become since being elevated to a managerial position. It appeared the promotion had gone to his head and changed his whole personality. He had become more critical and pompous, and acquired friends with whom she felt they had little in common. She didn't care for the superficiality of it all.

Having led such a sheltered life before she met Philip, she hadn't liked to question his superior knowledge. She had never drunk wine with a meal or tasted oriental dishes before they met, and felt a complete ignoramus, so had tried hard to be the sort of person he wanted her to be. She had taken cookery lessons, and read glossy magazines to see what was in fashion. But somewhere along the way, she had lost her own personality. Now she wanted to be herself again, unsophisticated and simple.

★ ★ ★

'Do you like country and western music, by any chance?' Joe asked her one fine morning as she was setting off for a walk.

'Oh yes, I certainly do. It's ages since I've been to a gig, though.' She smiled, thinking about what Philip would do if she asked him to take her to such an event.

'Well, I wondered if you'd care to join me at the local do this evening . . . unless you have something else on?' Joe said, rather nervously, looking somewhat embarrassed.

'I'd be delighted. As long as it's not a dressing-up type of occasion,' she replied. 'I didn't bring any fancy clothes on this trip.'

'Oh, no. The pub is just down the

road, and the group playing is a bunch of local lads, but they have quite a good reputation. I'll pick you up at eight then, shall I?'

Leanna smiled at the prospect of going out with someone. In the past, she'd not really gone out on many dates; she had always been shy and kept herself to herself. Though this wouldn't be a proper date as such. Although Joe was on his own — having been widowed some years previously, as she'd discovered during one of their chats — he was a lot older than her; getting on for retirement, probably. From what he'd told her already, she guessed he must be well into his fifties.

She was pleased she had washed her best jeans two days before, so they should be presentable, and she managed to find a clean T-shirt. She would need her thick sheepskin coat, since the evenings were getting quite cold, and a pair of stout walking shoes, as the lane was often wet and messy. She looked forward to the evening out and was ready in plenty of time.

'How long have you owned the campsite?' she asked as they strolled along the country lane, dodging the puddles.

Joe matched his stride to hers. 'The farm has been in the family for more years than I care to remember, but ten years ago it was my wife who suggested fencing off the one field and turning it into a caravan park. She'd read up about it in some magazine. I was dubious at first, but was talked into going along with the scheme. As it happens, it's proved to be a nice little earner.

'When Madge got ill, I found I couldn't manage to look after her, the campsite and the farm. Madge really wanted to stay at home. She hated the thought of hospitalisation, and I much preferred to look after her as long as I could. We'd known each other since we were five and first started school. She was the one and only girl for me, and we never spent a night apart all our married lives. Madge had always taken on the running of the campsite with very little help from me, so in the end I decided to let off the fields to adjacent farmers and kept the campsite going. It could still be a working farm if I decided to sell, but I manage to survive as it is, although I miss the animals.'

'I don't suppose you miss the early-morning starts, though, do you?'

He laughed and scratched his head. 'It actually took a while to get used to that, but I think it was the right decision. How about you? Are you taking what they call a sabbatical?'

She smiled, thinking it was a good term for what she was doing, and realised he was curious as to her being there on her own.

'I wouldn't call it that as such. A writer needs solitude, but I'm also wondering whether my husband, Philip, and I are actually compatible. You know the saying: 'Change the name but not the letter, change for worse and not for better'? Well, I'm wondering if that's what I've done.'

'I see. Marriage can be difficult. All I would say is, don't do anything too hasty.'

'Act in haste and repent at leisure, you mean?' She sighed. 'No, I won't. I just think we've lost our way a bit.'

'It happens,' he replied. 'Is there anyone you can talk to, for a bit of advice, like a sounding board? Someone who knows you well. What about your family?'

She shook her head. 'I have none. At least, none that I know about.'

'Oh? How come?'

She gave an embarrassed little chuckle. 'I'm an orphan. Poor little orphan Annie, that's me. It's a long story, but the short version is, my parents and brother were killed in one of those horrible motorway pile-ups.' She paused. 'I guess that's why I'm quite self-sufficient and happy with my own company. It's something I had to get used to.'

'That's tragic. You've had it tough for one so young. I can't imagine what it's like not having any close relatives.'

'You have family then?'

'Sure. I've a brother and sister, both with children. Unfortunately, Madge and I didn't have any of our own.' He paused. 'Surely you have some distant relatives somewhere, haven't you? I mean, nobody's ever totally alone.'

Leanna sighed. 'Well yes, possibly . . . Only, it's complicated. It was only after my family were killed that I discovered I was actually adopted. So was my brother, I think. I have no idea who my biological parents are.'

'Good heavens. That must have been traumatic on top of everything else.'

'You can say that again. I was really angry for a while, but then gradually came to see how my adoptive parents must have felt, perhaps never finding just the right moment to tell me. They did, after all, give my brother and me a wonderful childhood. I couldn't have asked for better.'

Fortunately they had arrived at the pub; and judging by the noise, the gig was about to start, so nothing else was said. Leanna was relieved. She hadn't spoken about her adoption for quite some time, and wasn't sure why she had said so much to Joe. Maybe because he was a stranger and she was feeling lonely. She certainly didn't want anyone feeling sorry for her. It always made her feel embarrassed.

Joe pushed a way through the crowd and managed to find her a window seat. While he was getting the drinks, she located a chair for him. She was taken aback by the large turnout in such a small village. She'd thought maybe Joe had been coerced into going to swell the numbers, but nothing could have been further from the truth. The place was heaving. Normally, she would have been cautious of such a sizeable gathering, but Joe soon put her at her ease and introduced her to some of his friends.

The entertainment was excellent foot-tapping music, and she thoroughly enjoyed the whole evening. Joe proved to be pleasant company. He didn't monopolise the conversation; and at times, egged on by his friendly neighbours, Leanna found him quite witty. The other locals were a sociable bunch, and she thought she would feel comfortable going there again on her own sometime, when she felt like a pub lunch.

One young man called Carl, the son of a local farmer, asked if she would like him to show her something of the locality, since she was there on her own. Leanna was somewhat taken aback by his attention and tried to let him down as gently as possible.

'I'm sorry, but I'm married.'

'Yes, Joe mentioned it,' Carl replied, with a shrug of his shoulders. 'But surely that doesn't stop you from going out and enjoying yourself. Like tonight, for example?'

She didn't know what to say to that, and blushed bright pink.

'How about a night at the cinema? Surely there's no harm in that?'

She had to agree that it sounded all right, and it would be nice to have an escort home after dark.

'I'll see what's on and let you know,' Carl said, getting up to leave. 'There's not a great deal of choice, as there's only one screen.'

★   ★   ★

The very next day, as Leanna was preparing her lunch, Carl presented himself at the door of the campervan.

'Hi,' he said. 'Something smells good.'

'It's only soup,' she said nervously. The more she had thought about her quick acquiescence to his suggestion the night before, the more she had regretted it in hindsight. She had spent ages trying to think up a polite reason to give for why she couldn't go out with him, but hadn't found anything suitable. She hated causing an upset and usually went out of her way to please people. This was the result, she thought ruefully — she was being persuaded to do something she would rather not do.

'I was just passing,' Carl said, 'and thought I'd let you know that *Where Eagles Dare* is on tonight. Fancy seeing it? It's a great film.'

Cautiously, she agreed, and said she would meet him in Whitby for a coffee before the show. Something niggled her, and she decided she would just see how things went. If necessary, she would pluck up the courage to walk home alone.

* * *

Actually, Carl was rather sweet. He bought her a box of chocolates and even asked if she would like an ice cream in the interval. She enjoyed the film, even though she had seen it before, and he insisted on seeing her home. He wouldn't take no for an answer. On the way, he regaled her with stories about his obnoxious brothers. Apparently he was the youngest of four, and was forever being tormented by his older siblings for being shy and somewhat reticent. That wasn't how he came across to her, but she didn't say so.

Leanna felt sorry for him in a way, so she agreed to another 'date'. This time he suggested walking part of the Cleveland Way — a recognised long-distance walk. He said he was free to go at the weekend, and mentioned catching the bus to Runswick Bay and walking back from there. Leanna hadn't a clue what she had let herself in for, but said she'd give it a go. She liked walking and loved the exercise. She only hoped the weather would be kind.

On Saturday she packed a substantial picnic lunch, which she thought she could share with Carl if necessary, and stuffed it in a duffel bag. She filled a flask with coffee and took a couple of cold drinks too. Somewhere she had read that it was important to keep drinking when out walking. She wished she had bought a map of the area, but it was too late now, so she would have to rely on Carl's knowledge of the route.

Saturday morning turned out to be sunny but breezy — ideal conditions, Carl informed her when they met up at the bus station. A single-decker bus arrived shortly afterwards and they clambered aboard. Leanna sat by the window and watched the passing scenery with absorbed fascination. It was all totally new territory for her. The bus duly dropped them off at the top of a steep hill, and spread out below was the most fantastic view Leanna had ever seen. Runswick Bay was an idyllic seaside village at the northern end of a glorious, curving, sandy bay.

Carl immediately urged her down a steep path to the beach and said it was just as well the tide was out. They had a little way to go along the beach before starting to climb a footpath heading south. She would have loved to have spent more time on the beach, as it looked very interesting; but Carl was eager to move on, saying they had a long way to go. They climbed up a steep rocky path, with Leanna gasping for breath, but on reaching the top she was enthralled. The scenery was stunning. She was so pleased Carl had brought her here, and only wished she had thought to bring her camera.

They walked on, mainly in single file due to the narrowness of the cliff path, leaving Leanna's mind to wander at will. They met very few people and little in the way of habitation, just the odd farmhouse here and there in the distance. Eventually she suggested it was time for some lunch, as her stomach was rumbling. Carl agreed and led her to a deserted spot overlooking a quiet bay. The weather had clouded over, and mist was forming out at sea. It was turning colder too. They sat in a hollow just below the cliff-top and Leanna poured the coffee. Carl had brought a few sandwiches, but seemed pleased when she said she had more than she wanted herself. It was so peaceful, and she was enjoying the quiet stillness until a few drops of rain landed on her.

'I'm glad I put my thickest sweater on,' she murmured, pulling up her anorak hood. 'I wonder if it'll last long.'

No sooner had she spoken when the rain started in earnest. A thundery downpour sent them scurrying for shelter in a nearby barn. The roof was ramshackle and the door hung off its hinges, but at least it was dry and provided some protection from the rain.

'Shame,' Leanna said, catching her breath and staring out at the unrelenting rain. 'I suppose we'd better call a halt and catch the bus. How far are we from the road?'

'It's miles away,' Carl said, sounding quite unconcerned. He threw himself down on some bales of hay. 'Might as well get comfortable. We may be here for quite a while. It doesn't look like letting up, and goodness knows when there'll be a bus anyway.'

Leanna was not at all pleased. 'I thought you said the path followed the coastline — but surely the road does that too, doesn't it?'

'Not near here,' he replied, with apparent disregard for her anxiety. 'Come on — come and make yourself comfortable,' he said, patting the hay. 'It's turned cold. We should huddle up together to keep warm. We don't want to risk hypothermia.'

'Don't be daft,' she snapped. 'If you're cold, jump about a bit. If the rain doesn't stop soon, I'm going to continue on my way. I don't care if I do get wet. I'm not staying here. It'll be dark before long.'

'Come on, Leanna. What's a hug and a kiss between friends?'

Leanna looked at him with a mixture of disbelief and anger. 'I can't believe you just said that! I told you, Carl — I'm married. I don't go in for affairs. If you chose not to listen, that's your own fault. I'm not staying here a moment longer.'

She stomped out of the barn, not caring in which direction she was heading; she just wanted to get as far away as possible. She eventually found a sort of track which she thought looked promising. It ran alongside a tall, overgrown hedge; and then, in a gap, she spotted a farmhouse. She headed towards it, thinking at least it was civilisation, but then noticed another, more distinct track, leading towards a road with traffic moving along it. Carl had lied — the main road wasn't more than half a mile away. Scrambling over a stile, she looked about her, wondering how long she would have to wait for a bus.

She decided she would start walking. It was too cold to stand around, even though the rain had dwindled to a fine drizzle. She was so angry with herself and Carl that she hardly noticed the dampness soaking through her anorak. But she hadn't gone far when a van driver pulled up alongside. It was a delivery van and smelled strongly of fish.

'Want a lift?' the driver asked. 'I'm going as far as Whitby, if you care to hop aboard.'

Leanna was so upset that she climbed in without a moment's hesitation. 'Thanks for stopping. I got caught in that last heavy shower on the Cleveland Way. I was going to catch the bus, but wasn't sure when or if there was one.'

'Not sure myself,' the van driver said, setting off again. 'At this time of year they're few and far between.'

He was a pleasant enough individual, if perhaps a little too chatty for Leanna's liking, but in no time at all they were descending the steep hill down from Lythe into the quaint village of Sandsend. Leanna was very relieved knowing she was in walking distance of her campervan. The van driver dropped her off on the harbour side in Whitby, and she smiled her thanks. She reflected ruefully that she certainly wouldn't be seeing Carl again, and would definitely listen to that niggling feeling in her gut next time.

Back at the campsite, she shrugged out of her wet clothes and went for a hot shower, hoping it would help overcome her feeling of depression and stupidity. How could she have been so dense? Before making herself an omelette, she decided to ring Philip. She so desperately needed some words of comfort to restore her morale. But there was no joy there. The phone rang and rang. Where was he? What was he doing?

7

A few days later, she was setting off for a walk when she saw Joe repairing a fence. He greeted her with a wave and strode over to chat.

'I've been thinking.' He paused and looked self-conscious. 'I hope you won't think me nosey or anything, but have you thought about trying to track down your relatives? I believe it's possible to check these things out now.'

Leanna shrugged. 'Obviously, from time to time it's crossed my mind, but I've always decided not to bother. Besides, I wouldn't know where to start.' She was about to walk on, but he continued.

'Why don't you have a look on the internet? That's what I'd do.'

She sighed and shrugged again, not quite sure what to say. 'I still wouldn't know how to go about it. Besides, I haven't got access to the internet at the moment, and I'm not very good with a computer. I mainly use mine as a glorified typewriter.'

Joe wasn't easily put off. He grinned. 'You could use mine. I've got a broadband link and I'd be happy to show you how to go about it. That is, if you don't think I'm being an interfering busybody.'

Leanna chewed her bottom lip. 'Well . . . I don't know . . . ' Then, seeing his hopeful expression, she relented and said, 'Okay, if you really think it's worthwhile. Thanks. What have I got to lose? But I don't want to be a nuisance, or wasting up your time; I don't have much information about them.'

That seemed to settle it. Joe looked pleased. 'No problem. My evenings are free these days. After Madge died, I set about tracing our family tree, and was surprised how many relatives we had that we didn't know about. I find it quite absorbing. I spend hours on the internet these days, more so than the old telly. Come round about seven and we'll see what we can find out. You never know . . . ' With that, he turned and walked back to work, whistling tunefully.

Now what have I done? Leanna sighed, not sure if she really wanted to know about her parentage. She'd had a happy enough childhood, so what difference would it make if she did indeed find something out about her biological parents? What if they were still alive? Would she want to meet them? They hadn't wanted her twenty-two years ago. She could do without this hassle, but she was committed now. Besides, Joe would soon give up the search when he realised it was a lost cause — she had so little to go on.

She strolled off down the lane deep in thought, and went for a much longer walk than usual. She found a disused railway track and ended up at a lovely little spot called Robin Hood's Bay. As she wended her way down the steep main thoroughfare, the cottages and passageways off to the side intrigued her. It was obviously a haunt of the smugglers in days gone by, and she knew she would have to return one day to learn more of its history. She was enchanted. It was a hodgepodge of houses, some precariously perched on the hillside.

She meandered down to the beach, past the fishermen's tackle and boats, and sat watching the dog walkers and their companions. A party of school children were examining the rock pools, eagerly shouting one to another. If she had children, she would love to bring them to such a place. It was so charmingly peaceful. She saw a woman with a toddler in bright red wellies splashing happily in a rock pool, laughing merrily. What a lovely picture they made. She felt quite envious.

After buying a sandwich and coffee at a small café, she wandered back, wondering what Philip would think if he could see her now. She wore a pair of scruffy trainers and her gardening jeans, and was decidedly windblown, but also happily carefree and relaxed.

At seven o'clock she presented herself at the back door of the farmhouse, not sure if she wanted to go through with the proposed search, unsure if she wanted to know anything about her birth parents. She was Leanna Wright with a husband to take care of her. What more did she want?

Joe opened the door promptly. 'Hi! Do come in.' He led her through to a small room off the kitchen which he obviously used as an office. 'I've already logged into the genealogy site I think most appropriate. Now, you will stop me if I become a bore, won't you? I've just become so fascinated with the subject, I'm really hooked. I needed something to fill in my time after Madge went, and . . . well, I just find it so absorbing.'

Leanna glanced around the room, thinking how comfortably untidy it was. It was clean but cluttered, and the carpet was almost threadbare, but it was homely. The shelves were stacked with books and paperwork, but the desk space was clear except for a scrap pad for making notes next to the telephone.

'It's very good of you to go to so much trouble on my behalf, but I'm not sure if it'll be very fruitful. I haven't much to go on, as I told you.'

'Well, to begin with, we'll jot down what you do know and take it from there. Now make yourself comfortable and tell me a little about yourself. That is, if you don't think I'm being too inquisitive. Whatever you tell me will go no further, I promise; and if you decide at any time to call a halt, then you only have to say. I know if it was me I would want to try to find out something about my parentage, but maybe you don't. It's just a shot in the dark at the moment.'

Leanna shuffled in her seat and took a deep breath. 'Okay. Well, as far as I know, I've always lived around York. When my adoptive parents, Ted and Mary Walker, were alive, we lived in a small village called Paxton, just outside

York. I had an older brother called Peter — also adopted, I suppose, although I don't know for certain. I don't even know if we were actually brother and sister; I guess we could have been. My father worked on a farm, so we lived in a tied cottage. Mother taught at the local primary school. We didn't have grandparents, or aunts and uncles; it was just Mum, Dad, Peter and me. We were just a simple, normal family, or so I thought. Then Peter was accepted to study at Warwick University. Mum and Dad were so thrilled. Dad took a day off work so Mum and he could take Peter down there before the start of term. We only had a small Mini, so there wasn't enough room for me to go too, what with all Peter's stuff he was taking; so I stayed at home. I've often thought it would've been better if . . . '

'No,' Joe said, kindly. 'Don't ever think like that.' Then he smiled. 'Sorry, I shouldn't have interrupted. So then what happened?'

'A woman in the village took me in — I'd always called her my aunt, although she wasn't really, she was just a close friend of the family. She was ever so kind. I don't know what I would've done without her. Anyway, to cut a long story short, I finished school, got a job, found a bedsit, and married Philip.'

'How did you find out you were adopted?'

'That was purely an accident. When I started clearing out the cottage, I came across lots of paperwork, like you do. I was about to set fire to it, but for some reason I decided to skim through it first. There was this sealed envelope. On the outside it had the date when I would be eighteen. Inside was this locket.' She opened it to show Joe the two tiny photos inside. 'I expect they're my biological parents, because they certainly aren't Ted and Mary. My aunt, when I bombarded her with questions, admitted she'd been told I was adopted, but she didn't know anything else. I believed her when she said she had no information to impart, and I had to leave it at that. Anyway, I had plenty of other problems to cope with and decided not to let it bother me.'

Joe asked lots of questions about where she went to school, what were her grandparents' names, and where did they live? Leanna told him what she could, and Joe checked it out. Leanna was surprised to learn Mary's parents had farmed not too far away from where she had grown up, in a small village called Goathland. Mary had apparently had a sister called Annabel, but Ted was an only child and had been brought up on a farm near Scarborough.

Over coffee they discussed possibilities, and Joe, with Leanna's agreement, said he would keep an eye on what responses they had from contacts they had made. Joe had asked for information about her relatives on various websites and was hopeful they would receive some replies before too long. Leanna couldn't see how it would work, but went along with Joe's enthusiastic approach.

She lay awake that night wondering if it was possible either of her biological parents were still alive, and whether she had brothers and sisters she'd never known about. Did she really want to know anyway, after all this time? Wouldn't it better to let the past stay in the past? She had, of course, often wondered why she had been put out for adoption. Had her mother died in childbirth? Had she been too young? Underage, even? Leanna had wondered about many different scenarios, but the thought she came back to most often was that she just hadn't been wanted.

Two days later, Joe knocked on her door.

'You've had some hits,' he said, looking very pleased with himself.

'What do you mean, hits?'

'Responses from possible relations. Two I don't think are relevant, but the third is a woman here in Yorkshire, and

I think it may be worth chasing up.'

Leanna accompanied him to the farmhouse and stared at the screen.

'My name is Elsie Jones and I have lived in Yorkshire all my life. I had a baby girl 22 years ago, but I was unwell and unable to take care of her, so she was adopted. I lost touch with her and have been desperately trying to trace her ever since. I called her Anne, but I'm not sure if her adoptive parents changed her name.'

'What do you think I should do?' Leanna murmured.

'There's no harm in following it up,' Joe said. 'She just may be your long-lost mother, but you'll never know unless you check it out.'

'She doesn't say where she lives. Yorkshire is a big county.'

Joe chuckled. 'You're not committing yourself to anything. She won't even know where you are unless you tell her.'

Leanna gulped. 'It's just so sudden.

I'm a bit apprehensive of course, but like you say, nothing ventured . . . '

'Look, come and use the computer whenever you want. I'd just love you to find some relative, no matter how distant. Even if they live on the other side of the world and you correspond by email. It'd make you feel not quite so alone, wouldn't it?'

Leanna thanked him profusely. She had to admit to becoming quite addicted to the search. However, several emails later she concluded Elsie and herself were not related. They parted amicably enough, each hoping the other found what they were looking for eventually. Joe apologised for getting her hopes up, but Leanna told him she really wasn't upset, and she appreciated his thoughtfulness.

*   *   *

Leanna got into a routine of a brisk walk to the beach early each morning. It was where she could do most of her thinking, and now she had plenty to think about. Firstly, was she still in love with Philip, and did she want to remain married? Secondly, her novel had taken a back seat while she trawled the internet in search of information about her past. Now she really needed to make more progress with her writing. She would love to have the novel completed before her return, if for no other reason than to show Philip she hadn't been wasting her time.

'Hello, kindred spirit.'

Leanna jerked round and almost fell over a small dog intent on jumping up at her. Its owner was a tall, fair-haired individual with rakish good looks. 'Sorry, I didn't mean to make you jump. I've seen you here so often that I feel I know you.'

Leanna frowned. 'Sorry, I was lost in thought.'

'Yes, I could see that. You often are. You were frowning as if you weren't very happy about something, and I wondered if I could help. Perhaps a coffee at the café yonder might do the trick? And maybe a bacon sandwich, too!'

She relented and smiled. She wouldn't let her escapade with Carl put her off all friendly overtures. She was ready for a coffee anyway. She bent down to have her hand sniffed by the dog. 'Sure, why not? I often call in there. It has such a lovely view.'

As they strolled towards the café, she explained one of her conundrums. 'I'm writing a novel and have a problem with one of the characters, which I can't see round as yet. But I will, given time.' She laughed to cover her embarrassment. 'What's your excuse?'

'No excuse; I just like walking along the beach, especially first thing in the morning while it's quiet. Rover does too. I'm Alex, by the way. Alex Grayson at your service, madam.' He had a gorgeous voice. Could have been an actor, she thought. She speculated about his age, but could only guess at anything from late thirties to fifty. She thought maybe he looked younger than he really was because of the way he dressed and his boyish hairstyle.

She laughed. 'Leanna Wright. So what do you do, Mr Grayson?'

He chuckled. 'Call me Alex. Mr Grayson sounds unfriendly. To earn an honest crust, you mean? Well, I'm an artist, for my sins. I have a gallery in town, which is where I should be right now, but I'm sure my assistant is more than capable of handling any prospective customer who may be browsing my lowly establishment. She has more of a head for the financial side of things than I do, and business is slow at this time of year. I sometimes think it'd be best if I shut up shop for the winter months.'

Leanna enjoyed the next half-hour chatting to him, and was sorry when he decided he ought to be making tracks. 'Ciao! See you tomorrow then, Leanna, weather permitting. Your turn to pay.'

For the next few mornings they met up and retired to the café for a coffee and chat. Leanna, at one stage, mentioned some of the other problems that were nagging her, and Alex proved to be a helpful sounding board.

'Why don't I take you out for dinner this evening?' he said as he was leaving on the Friday morning. 'I know a charming little Italian restaurant. You like Italian food?'

Leanna smiled. 'Well, yes . . . '

'Good, that's a date. I'll pick you up at seven.' And he was gone before she could refuse.

Leanna's heart raced. What on earth had possessed her? She knew nothing about the man, and yet she had agreed to have dinner with him — a perfect stranger. She must have taken leave of her senses. Hadn't she learned anything from the fiasco with Carl?

Hurrying back to the campervan, she contemplated contacting Alex and pleading a just-remembered prior engagement, but didn't know where to find him. She couldn't traipse all round Whitby looking for his art gallery. She had other things to worry about too. What could she possibly wear? She hadn't brought clothes for such an occasion, and didn't want to raid her funds too heavily. She did momentarily consider her sundress, but decided it really wasn't right. There was nothing else for it but to scour the charity shops again to find something appropriate.

The assistants were extremely helpful since she had bought and recycled lots of paperbacks in the past few weeks. They showed her various possibilities, but nothing attracted her, and she had almost given up hope of finding something suitable. She had visited just about every charity shop in the town, and was prepared to settle for trousers and a simple top, when she finally located a smart, green, patterned sheath dress tucked away in a corner. It had three quarter length sleeves and a low rounded neckline.

'Try it on,' the assistant urged her. 'It's your colour and quite a bargain.'

Leanna headed for the tiny cubicle feeling embarrassed. She hated shopping for clothes, and the pantomime of trying them on behind a flimsy curtain. However, she was pleased to see it fitted reasonably well, although it was slightly longer than she would have wished.

'Yes, I'll take it,' she told the assistant. 'Now all I need is a pair of shoes or sandals, and a shawl or something, and I'm made up.'

'The only shoes we have that might suit are these,' the assistant said, rummaging on the bottom shelf. She produced a pair of very high-heeled open-toed shoes.

Leanna shook her head in despair. 'Gosh, I've never worn anything so high.' She tried them on and they fitted. 'Oh well, I only hope I don't have far to walk,' she said with a grimace.

'And I'm sure we have a shawl here somewhere; it's beige,' the assistant continued, digging in a drawer behind the counter. 'Aha! Here we go. It wouldn't look too out of place. What do you think?'

'Fine. What do I owe you?' Leanna just wanted to escape, and prepare for the evening. She was highly delighted at how little the whole ensemble had cost, though.

By the evening, she was extremely nervous and ready miles too early, so sat re-reading her manuscript, and making a few minor alterations. She was so engrossed in her work she nearly missed hearing the car pulling up on the road outside. She carefully walked out to meet him, her high heels making it rather tricky as they sank into the soft earth.

'Hello,' he said and gave a whistle of appreciation. 'I would never have recognised you as the beach belle I've been having coffee with each morning.'

She dipped a curtsey. 'Thank you, kind sir. Much appreciated.'

'I assume this is your natural colour,' he said, indicating her freshly washed hair. 'So why the wig? Your hair is a gorgeous colour. Too beautiful to hide.'

'Didn't I tell you, I'm here incognito?' she said with a laugh to cover up her embarrassment. 'I'll explain later.'

He settled her in the passenger seat

of his large, expensive saloon car and drove smoothly off. Leanna was puzzled and a little alarmed when he turned south and didn't head for Whitby.

Seeing her apprehension, he laughed. 'I didn't say where I was taking you, did I?'

'No,' she replied, nervously.

He patted her hand and smiled. 'Relax. I'm not kidnapping you. I know there are perfectly good restaurants in Whitby, but I happen to prefer one particular one in Scarborough. It's only twenty miles, so settle back and enjoy the ride. I don't often dine out with a charming lady companion, so I thought we should make a pleasant evening of it. Or we could go back and get some fish and chips on the pier,' he said, with a grin.

She was beginning to feel less anxious, but a little guilty. Philip would definitely not approve; but what the heck.

'Much as I do like fish and chips,' she said, 'I'm happy to go along with your suggestion. I haven't been to Scarborough for donkey's years. I think I was taken there in a minibus with the Sunday school. I remember being absolutely taken aback when I saw the sea for the first time. It must be nice to live by the sea, I think.'

He smiled and nodded. 'Scarborough is a beautiful town, well worth exploring when you have the time. It was the first seaside resort in this country, you know. It's bigger and busier than Whitby, and definitely has lots that would interest you.'

They came over the brow of a hill and she could see the lights twinkling up ahead. It hadn't taken them long; Alex drove so smoothly and unobtrusively. She wished she could be so accomplished. He slowed as they approached the outskirts.

'Not far now. I think you'll like Angelina's.'

There was little traffic, and in what seemed like no time at all he was parking right outside the restaurant. It looked very attractive; small and welcoming rather than large and flashy, like she might have expected if she'd been with Philip. As they entered, she admired the subdued lighting and intimate booths, intriguing pictures on the walls, and tasteful choice of music playing in the background. It had a pleasant ambience. Alex had booked, so they were shown immediately to their table in a cosy corner. Leanne felt suddenly self-conscious and glanced round at the other clientele for fear of meeting someone she recognised. For all she knew, the Fieldings or Philip's other friends could frequent such a place. York wasn't so far away. Fortunately, she didn't see anyone she recognised. Relaxing slightly, she turned her attention to the menu the waiter handed her. Oh gosh, she thought, it was a very extensive choice as well as being expensive.

'It's quite a comprehensive menu, isn't it?' Alex said. 'If it's any help, I can definitely recommend the Avocado con Gamberetti, and perhaps the Suprema di Pollo Gratinato to follow.'

She smiled her gratitude. 'Sounds

good to me,' she replied, hoping she would be able to eat whatever it was she had ordered.

Alex was an entertaining character and soon had her explaining about her wish for anonymity. She found she was unburdening herself more than she usually would to a relative stranger. She explained about the dinner party and the challenge she had undertaken, which required her to be incognito. He found it amusing and said he didn't think he could exist on so little.

'That's no problem,' Leanna said. 'When I left school I lived in a pokey bedsit with shared facilities, and had little left each week to live on once I'd paid the rent.'

He stretched across and covered her hand, his long tapering fingers squeezing hers.

'That must have been tough. I know my family can be a pain at times, but really I wouldn't want to be without them.'

She grimaced. 'The thing that's

worrying me now is I don't know if I want to find out about my real parents,' she said, having expounded about her search for relatives. 'Joe has gone to so much trouble on my behalf, and at times I get quite excited, but then I have my down moments. I feel it would be better to leave well alone. There are so many 'what if's. I'm all muddled up.'

'I see your point, my dear. I'm not sure if I would want to pursue it if I were in your shoes. For myself, I would follow up all enquiries from a distance, and decide later if I wished to make contact. That way you have nothing to lose and perhaps a lot to gain. That's the beauty of the internet — its anonymity.'

She grinned. 'Yes, you're right. I am curious, naturally, and I have made some progress. I have quite a few possible lines of enquiry to follow up. I'm finding it interesting, in a way. Actually, I've been tracing my husband's ancestors too. I do believe I have unearthed a distant relative of his who was sent out to Australia as a convict. I'm not sure I should mention him to Philip!'

When they were at the coffee stage, Leanna looked across at Alex, feeling comfortable and carefree. The meal had been superb and Alex was excellent company.

'So far this evening we've talked all about me,' she said, 'but I know absolutely nothing about you.'

He raised an eyebrow. 'Beginning to have doubts about my integrity?'

'Oh no,' she replied, with a chuckle. 'Just curious, that's all.'

'What do you wish to know?'

'Oh, you know. Where were you born, are you married, that sort of thing.'

'I see. Well, you've probably realised I am almost old enough to be your father. I was born near Whitby thirty-eight years ago, and yes, I have been married, but it didn't work out so I'm currently footloose and fancy free. I'm the youngest of three. I have an older sister, who is married and lives in

London, and a recluse of a brother living in France. My parents are still alive and kicking, and occasionally give me a hard time because I haven't found a suitable wife or produced more grandchildren for them.'

She chuckled again, trying to remember how much wine she'd had. She definitely felt slightly tipsy. 'Your sister has children?'

'Oh yes. Three young hooligans who spend their summer holidays terrorising me. They allegedly come to see their grandparents, but I am delegated to keep them out of mischief. Of course, they are adored by my parents, and my sister believes they are absolute little innocents.'

'Do I take it you're not particularly interested in children?'

'Heaven forbid. They're all right when they're first born, but as soon as they can crawl they are nothing but a disaster.'

'It's just as well you and your ex didn't have any then.' She frowned.

'Why do you say your brother is a recluse?'

He leaned back in his chair, thoughtfully. 'Harry. He is the talented one of the family. He's a damned fine artist, although he always wanted to become a teacher. He would have made good one, too. He has patience, which is something I lack. I say I'm an artist, but Harry has more talent in his little finger than I have in the whole of my body. Anyway, one snowy Christmas he had an accident on the notorious Saltersgate Bank. Do you know it?'

'Oh yes. I must say, I was rather apprehensive coming down it.'

'It can be treacherous, especially in winter. Harry was on his way home when his motorbike skidded off the road. The accident left him confined to a wheelchair, so he gave up his career and went to live in France. He said he wanted to be as far away from civilisation as he could get. He couldn't bear the pitying looks from all and sundry?'

'How awful. But surely he comes back to see your parents occasionally?'

'No. Harry's not set foot in this country in twenty years. He married his girlfriend, Bel, and she's looked after him ever since. We — that is, my parents and I — pop over to see them from time to time, but they lost touch with all their friends. However, they seem happy enough.'

'So you've lived all your life in or near Whitby?' Leanna said, to change the subject.

'Hmm. I did consider sailing off into the far blue yonder at one time, but I'm too lazy and think yachts are too much like hard work. My parents have one down in the harbour, but it's not stirred further than Robin Hood's Bay for ages. I'm with my ex on that one — she wanted to sail round the Greek Isles, but she wanted to do it the sensible way: with a crew to look after you.'

'I've never been on a yacht,' Leanna said, thoughtfully.

'Like to?'

She shook her head. 'I'd probably be seasick. I didn't travel well when we crossed the channel on a ferry a couple of years back. I was told it was calm as a mill pond, so I don't think I'd be a very good sailor.'

He glanced at his watch. 'I think we'd better be going if I'm to get you home before the witching hour.'

He paid the bill and took her by the arm to guide her back to the car. She was glad of his support because she found the shoes difficult to walk in — or was it that she was ever so slightly intoxicated?

On the way home she asked why his marriage hadn't worked out.

'Nothing specific, it was just one of those things. If you were to press me, I would say we were both too young, had different interests, different expectations. Rose was a model, so enjoyed being in the limelight and thought Whitby might as well have been the backside of the moon. For a time, we did have a flat in London — to please her — but I couldn't tolerate her so-called friends. I thought being part of the London scene would be exhilarating, and I suppose to start with it was, but eventually I saw how superficial the life was. Rose liked nothing better than to party, but to me it seemed so stupid spending time and money at these events, pretending you were delighted to see everybody, when the truth was you didn't recognise most of the people from Adam.

'Living in London seemed almost frantic with stress and pressure, and unless one was prepared to accept that lifestyle, it just became isolating. No, Whitby suits me very well. I guess I am plain lazy. I don't see why one should put up with all the hassle of city life. I make sufficient for my needs and enjoy a tranquil lifestyle without jumping through hoops trying to keep up with the affluent, swanky Joneses.'

'Oh, I couldn't agree more with your philosophy,' Leanna said enthusiastically. 'I wish my husband could see that. He seems obsessed with being seen in all the right places, socialising with all the right people, but to be truthful, I think it makes him look stupid.'

'So that was why you accepted the challenge — to take time out to review your marriage?' Alex said, softly.

'I suppose so. The thing is, I do still love Philip — at least the Philip I married. Unfortunately, he's changed. I think we both have. I thought time apart might help us focus on what is important to each of us.'

He didn't reply, but drove leisurely back to Whitby, where they arrived safely a little after eleven o'clock.

Leanna thanked him for a pleasant evening, but as she got out of the car, he frowned.

'You know, something has been bothering me ever since I first saw you all dressed up this evening. I have definitely seen you somewhere before, or if not you, someone very like you — and I don't mean down on the beach. I shall have sleepless nights until I remember where.'

She chuckled. 'Goodnight, Alex. Thank you ever so much for a lovely evening.'

'See you down on the beach tomorrow, weather permitting,' he replied with a laugh and motored off.

8

Philip was getting more and more anxious. He knew Leanna was more than capable of looking after herself, but he was still worried. He wondered why she hadn't replied to the messages he'd left on her phone. Perhaps she hadn't read them. He wished now they had never gone to the damned dinner party. Well, it was too late, the damage was done. He only hoped Leanna was coping in her usual capable manner and that when she returned they could get back to how they had been when they were first married. Those had been good times.

He had toured all round the Yorkshire moors and coast looking for the campervan, and checked most of the caravan sites, but nobody had seen or heard of her. He'd telephoned a few too, but it still took a lot of time since some of the sites were small, just grassy fields in some cases, and not registered. He tried to put himself in her shoes but it didn't help. Leanna was a much more organised person than him. She was so much more able, as his mother kept reminding him.

When he met Henry one evening, he gathered the others had had the same result. Zilch. It was if she had simply disappeared into thin air. He hoped she hadn't gone abroad; she really wasn't that experienced a driver, and who knows what trouble she might find herself in. God, he wished she would just ring and let him know she was all right. One thought kept crossing his mind. Had she gone looking for her real parents? She didn't mention them much, but it was a possibility.

With that in mind, he had spent some time touring round her childhood village of Paxton on the off chance she was there. He talked to the villagers and the landlord at the pub, but nobody had seen her. He did consider making enquiries about her heritage on the web, but she hadn't told him enough to go on. She was such a private person.

He wondered if Leanna had been feeling broody. They hadn't actually talked about starting a family, but now the idea seemed very appealing. He knew his parents would welcome grandchildren. His father was improving now, and spending a little time each day at the office. He congratulated Philip on his handling of things while he had been incapacitated and said Philip was a changed man. Oh, he really needed to talk to Leanna; there was so much he wanted to talk to her about! So much they ought to have talked about already. He wandered round the house and ended up in the small back bedroom. They had, at one time, thought about making it an office. It was cluttered with miscellaneous items that needed to be found homes, but it would make an ideal nursery. It would be fun decorating it together. Where had the fun gone from their lives? They used to laugh and joke about trivial things. He'd love to hear her happy laughter again.

He recalled how they had met and how touched he had been when he discovered her sad situation. He'd been delivering some stationery to the estate agents where she was working, and thought how charming she looked. He made a point of being outside when she was leaving and asked if she would like a lift. Three months later, they were married. He just knew they were right for each other, and she seemed to think the same. The age gap didn't seem to matter; she was mature for her years, and the loss of her family made him want to take care of her. He was delighted she got on so well with his parents — his mother especially.

He thought again how surprised she had been when he said he wanted her to be a full-time housewife, and there was no need for her to go out to work. Perhaps he had been selfish, but he looked forward to seeing her there when he returned home from the office. Just like his mother had always been home whenever he came back from school. He felt proud he could provide for Leanna so well. There was no need for her to slave away at some poorly paid job.

He looked around the house and realised how homely she had made it, but it wasn't the same without her presence. He missed her dreadfully. Just recalling their honeymoon in France brought tears to his eyes. She had never been abroad before and had been so thrilled just obtaining her passport. When she came home, and Christmas was over, he fully intended taking her abroad again. They could perhaps go skiing, or if she preferred it, some warm, sunny, beach resort. Just have some time out together. With any luck, Dad would be able to cope by then.

9

The café was quiet and they sat at a window table enjoying the view. Leanna felt comfortable in Alex's company and it was nice to have someone to talk to. She was mulling over what she should buy for lunch when he leaned across and whispered conspiratorially to her.

'I'm dying to show you something,' he said. 'Can you drop by the gallery sometime?'

'Sure,' she said, cautiously. 'But why?'

'You know I said you reminded me of someone. Well, now I know who. It was the early hours of the morning when it came to me.'

'So I have a double, do I?' she said, with a laugh. 'Tell me more.'

He shook his head. 'You'll have to come and see for yourself.'

The sense of mystery left Leanna

feeling compelled to go and see what he had found.

'No time like the present,' she said, getting to her feet. 'Let's go. I've some shopping to do in town anyway.'

They walked along the quayside and up the main street, with Alex greeting people everywhere. Leanna thought how nice it must be to be recognised like that, but of course, he'd lived here all his life. Along the narrow pavements he took her arm and guided her into a side street. She was now in a part of Whitby she hadn't so far investigated, and she was beginning to wonder if she would find her way back. His gallery, when they arrived, was a pleasant, spacious affair, but there weren't many paintings on view. Leanna wasn't sure if that meant there weren't many to sell or whether it was a selling technique in itself. She was glad she hadn't mentioned her own pitiful attempts, and admitted only to not understanding art. She said she felt out of her depth when wandering round galleries.

'You're not alone in that,' he replied. 'Now come this way, and see what I've got to show you.' He ushered her through to the rear of the shop, ignoring his assistant who glanced up from a desk in the corner. The back room was small, but had a large window looking out onto an alleyway. Alex went over to an easel in the corner and threw back the cover. 'Now, what do you think? That is strangely like you, isn't it?'

Leanna didn't know what to say. She was stunned. The likeness was uncanny, even down to the auburn hair. Her own hair was lighter, and the eyes in the picture were green — a wonderful, deep, emerald green — but other than that, it was like looking in a mirror.

'Who is she?' she whispered, not taking her eyes off the painting.

'Dunno.' He propped himself up against the windowsill and folded his arms. 'Like I said before, Harry has bucket loads more talent than me. That is one of his paintings.'

'Harry's your brother who lives in

France, right? It's his work? Is there a date or title or anything?'

'Sorry, no. I think it was unfinished.'

'If it was before he left to live in France, it would have been painted twenty or so years ago, then? That's much before my time, I hope you realise,' she said with an embarrassed laugh.

He nodded. 'Of course, unless you are a reincarnation. Anyway, that's one mystery solved.'

'Maybe for you, but not for me,' Leanna murmured, rather disturbed by the painting. 'I wonder who she is. She could be my double, except I have blue eyes, and I've never owned a dress like she's wearing. She's beautiful though, isn't she? He's captured a sort of wistful expression, I think.'

'Harry isn't a hoarder like me, so although he didn't take much with him when he went, he also didn't leave much in the way of possessions or anything here. He just upped and left, never to return. My mother may remember something relevant. I'll ask her, although after all this time I wouldn't bank on it.'

Leanna could hardly tear herself away. She had a feeling it was going to be very important to her, but she had no idea why.

'Thank you for showing it to me, Alex.' Tearing her eyes away from the painting, she asked, 'Is it for sale?' She wasn't sure if she could afford it straight-away, but perhaps she could leave a deposit. Then she wished she had never asked, because it may be very valuable and he could feel awkward about asking for its true price. 'Sorry, I shouldn't have asked,' she said hurriedly. 'I'd best be off.'

Alex scratched his head. 'I hadn't thought . . . I'll have to talk to my parents, obviously. They may wish to keep it for sentimental reasons, although I don't know why, as it's been stuck in the attic all these years. It was pure chance I spotted it recently. You know what parents are like . . . oh! Sorry,' he murmured, when he realised his gaffe.

Leanna couldn't get over the startling

likeness. Was she about to discover her mother? Was it possible Alex's brother held the key? That would be quite a coincidence, but coincidences happened. Maybe the gods were smiling on her today.

★ ★ ★

Later that day, Alex called at the campervan to see her. 'Can I come in?'

Leanna, somewhat startled, not being used to callers, waved her hand in welcome.

'Of course. Welcome to my humble abode. Can I make you a coffee? It's instant, I'm afraid.'

Alex glanced about before perching on one of the side seats. 'No thanks. Leanna, I think you should sit down. I have some amazing news for you.' He looked both serious and excited.

She frowned and sat opposite him. 'What is it? What's wrong?'

'Nothing's wrong. It's just something so staggeringly unbelievable.'

'For crying out loud! What is? It's about the picture isn't it?'

He nodded his head and beamed. He leaned across and covered her hands with his. 'It's just possible you and me . . . or should it be you and I . . . ? Anyway, we just might be related to each other.'

Leanna gasped. 'How do you mean?'

He sat back. 'I was unsettled; I don't like unresolved mysteries, so I went to see my folks after you left this morning. I bundled the painting in the car and took it with me. When I showed it to my mother she gave me quite a rollicking, and told me I needed my head examined. Apparently the portrait is of my sister-in-law, Bel. Harry's wife. I don't know why I hadn't twigged it for myself, but of course, she's aged somewhat, having had quite a tough life these last twenty years. Looking after Henry hasn't been easy. I'd forgotten how she used to look — not that I was around much in those days to notice. I only saw her a couple of times before they went to live in France.'

Leanna stared dumbfounded. Slowly she said, 'You're thinking maybe Bel is my mother?'

He nodded his head, grinning from ear to ear. 'Isn't that exciting? Definitely needs checking out, don't you think?'

'But . . . but . . . ' she stuttered. 'You said they live in France.'

He laughed. 'Yes, that's right. It's not the other side of the world you know. We could easily pop over to see them.'

Leanna sighed, thinking it was easy for him to say but to her it may as well be the other side of the world.

'Look,' he said, 'Mother suggested I make the trip to see my brother. My parents were going to go, like they always do for his birthday, but Father isn't too grand so she's asked me to go instead. I thought you could come with me.'

'I can't go to France,' she squeaked.

'Why not?'

'It's just . . . Well . . . Why don't we write, or phone?'

'No telephone. I told you, they have a very primitive lifestyle. No telephone. No television. They keep a few chickens and the odd goat, I believe. I haven't been for a long time, but I don't suppose things have changed much. Come with me, Leanna. Where's your spirit of adventure? We'll drive down to Portsmouth to catch the overnight ferry. My brother lives in a small village not too far from Caen, so it's quite convenient.'

'But I can't just turn up out of the blue. What will they think? It could all just be a pure coincidence. Bel might not have anything to do with me at all. I couldn't . . .'

He leaned across and took hold of her hands that were busy twisting a handkerchief into knots.

'Leanna, trust me. I'll make sure nobody gets hurt. This will be just a trip to see my brother for his birthday. You can say you're along for the ride, and we'll see what materialises. Think of it as a mini holiday. You do trust me don't you? I wouldn't do anything to cause you a problem, I promise. Like I said, I don't like mysteries, and I'd like to resolve this, one way or another. You would too, wouldn't you?'

She nodded. 'I really don't know what's best. I never thought . . . It's all so sudden.' She shook her head. 'Surely . . . ' Then she unearthed the locket she nearly always wore. She opened it and gazed at the photos. They were quite faded and somewhat indistinct. 'Do . . . do you recognise them?' she asked handing Alex the locket. 'I thought they must be my parents.'

He looked at them for what seemed like a long time before he nodded. 'Yes . . . Yes, I really do think that is my brother and his wife.'

★ ★ ★

Two days later they were on their way. Leanna couldn't believe how quickly Alex had managed to talk her into this latest development. She was certainly glad she hadn't done as Moira suggested and swapped passports. She only hoped she had sufficient funds for whatever she needed. Going abroad sounded expensive, although Alex wouldn't hear of her paying for the ferry tickets or even a contribution towards the petrol cost.

He picked her up early, and they drove south, bypassing York. Soon, they were on the motorway. She sank back against the soft leather seat, thinking she may as well do as Alex said and relax. She was on her way to who knew what. She was in his hands. All this had started with a simple challenge over a dinner table, but who knew where it would end?

10

'Not far now,' Alex said. 'Don't worry. Two days, three at the most, and you'll be back in your own little campervan, safe and sound.'

'I should have brought a present,' Leanna said with a frown. 'You said it's your brother's birthday. Could we stop and buy him a bottle of wine or something?'

He shook his head and smiled. 'All taken care of, now relax will you?'

How could she relax when she may be about to come face to face with her parents? Would they recognise her? What was she to say? *Hi, I'm Leanna. Remember me? The daughter you gave away at birth?* Of course she couldn't. She didn't want to upset them, especially as she didn't know the truth yet. She just wanted . . . What did she want? To understand what had led them to give her away — if indeed they were her parents. There was obviously some doubt about that, but it was best to be prepared. What had been so terrible they couldn't have kept her? The Graysons sounded fairly well off, so surely would have helped out financially, at least to start with. They would be her grandparents, after all. Grandparents. Gosh. She hadn't thought about the other relatives she would inherit if it turned out she was related to Bel and Harry. *Whatever am I doing here? This is a mistake.*

Alex drove carefully through a small village, avoiding chickens wandering hither and thither, and after about a mile or so, slowed right down to creep the car along a rutted track, before pulling up near a rickety gate.

'This is as far as we go. The house is up there.'

Leanna wiped her sweating palms on her trousers.

'You go and say hello. I'll wait here.'

'Are you sure?' he said, gazing sympathetically at her strained face. 'All right.

I'll be back in a minute. Don't go any-where.'

She choked back a laugh. She was in a foreign country, miles from anywhere, with little money. Where could she go?

Alex got out of the car and wandered up the path, hands in pockets, and soon disappeared from sight. Leanna gazed after him, anxiously awaiting his return. She was preparing herself for a huge disap-pointment. This was all a horrible mistake. She shouldn't have come. She shouldn't have been so easily talked into it. Now she was so close, she felt terribly scared.

She heard a car drawing up nearby and saw a woman extract herself from the passenger seat, along with several shopping bags. She approached, having waved good bye to the driver, took one look at Leanna and swore.

'You,' she said, her face turning a pasty shade of grey. She looked about to faint. 'Why now? What took you so long?' she snapped.

Leanna stepped out of the car dumb-founded. 'I beg your pardon?'

The woman peered at her. 'You're Leanna, aren't you?'

Leanna nodded, hardly daring to breathe.

'You've had over four years to come. So why now?' The woman seemed to be having difficulty breathing and was wheezing badly.

Leanna stared at her. There was something familiar about her. She could possibly be the woman in the painting. Her greying hair was scooped back in an untidy bun, and her face was devoid of make-up. She looked to be around fifty years old, she guessed. Leanna surmised this was Bel — Harry's wife. Could she possibly be her mother? She seemed to know her name.

At that moment, Alex reappeared. He smiled at the woman and kissed her on both cheeks. 'Surprise, surprise, Bel. We've dropped in to wish Harry happy birthday.'

'Why?' Bel said again to Leanna. 'Why now?'

Leanna bit her lip, then straightened her back, determined to remain calm.

'If you are my real mother then I've come to find out why you gave me away. I would have thought . . . '

'Surely Mary told you,' Bel snapped, her shoulders drooping wearily.

'Told me what?'

Alex looked from one to the other, but said nothing, clearly mystified.

Bel shook her head and put the shopping bags on the ground. She took a deep breath. 'I see you have the locket. I guess Mary gave you it when you were eighteen. So she would also have told you why you were adopted.'

'Shouldn't we go inside and discuss this with Harry?' Alex said, quietly retrieving the shopping and heading back up the path.

Bel watched him go, but stood her ground. She was waiting for an answer.

'Mary died over six years ago,' Leanna said, softly. 'She told me nothing. I found this locket in an envelope when I was clearing out the house.'

'Mary's dead?' Bel whispered, tears glistening.

146

Leanna nodded. 'Yes. Along with Ted, and my brother, Peter. It was a car accident.'

Bel wiped a hand over her forehead. 'This wasn't supposed to happen. Why wasn't I informed?' She stumped off after Alex, muttering inaudibly.

Leanna thought she had better follow suit. She walked slowly, fearful of what lay ahead.

The farmhouse was small but reasonably tidy. Leanna stepped into the hallway and, hearing voices from a room at the end, walked towards it.

Alex spotted her and took her by the arm. 'Leanna, love, come and meet Harry.'

Leanna smiled wanly at the man in the wheelchair sitting by a cosy fire.

'Hello,' she said, cautiously. 'Many happy returns of the day.'

Harry Grayson stared at her for what seemed like several minutes. Then he turned his gaze on his wife, his eyebrows raised questioningly.

'I'm sorry, Harry. It wasn't supposed

to happen like this. I should have told you everything a long time ago. I'm so sorry.'

'Perhaps we should all sit down and you can tell us now,' Harry said, quietly, clearly stunned.

Alex pulled out a chair for Leanna, and sat down next to her. Bel subsided onto a chair at the opposite side of the room. She was clearly distraught.

'I'm so sorry. So very sorry.' She faced Harry and took a deep breath. 'This all began with Mary, my sister.'

Leanna gave a gasp — Bel was Mary's sister? So this was her Aunt Annabel — wait, no! If Bel was her mother then ... the woman she thought had been her mother had really been her aunt?

Bel looked at her as if she knew what was going through Leanna's mind, and nodded slightly, before continuing.

'You remember she couldn't have children; they'd adopted Peter.'

Harry nodded, but remained silent.

'Oh Harry, that night you had your

accident — you were on your way to tell your parents about us, and that we were going to get married, remember? But afterwards . . . you were in hospital for months. I didn't know if you were going to live even, so when . . . when I discovered I was pregnant, I couldn't discuss it with you. You were in such bad shape you wouldn't have known what I was talking about. I hadn't been introduced to your parents, so I couldn't talk to them. I saw them from time to time when I visited you but . . . well . . . they didn't know about us. I felt shut out. Not wanted. I just didn't know what to do for the best. I needed to talk to someone who would understand.

'I knew there was no way I could cope alone, so I did what I thought was for the best. I knew Mary wanted a sibling for Peter, and I . . . I thought at least I would know our child had a good home.'

'Why didn't you tell me later, when I recovered?' Harry asked in a quiet, controlled voice.

'Because it was too late. I'd already told Mary she could have my baby.'

'Our baby.'

'Yes, of course. Our baby.'

'Leanna, I'm sorry. This must be very distressing for you,' Harry said, turning to Leanna. 'If you'll bear with us, perhaps it would be as well if we heard the whole story, don't you think?'

Leanna nodded. 'Yes, of course.' She was having great difficulty in taking it all in. Alex stared at the floor, not saying a word.

'Well, Bel? Please continue. What did you do?' Harry snapped.

Bel seemed to have recovered her composure. She lifted her head up and held her arms across her chest.

'I stayed at my flat in York for a while, but then the lease ran out and I had to go to stay with Mary and Ted. They took care of me, and when Leanna was born I told them as far as I was concerned they had to think of Leanna as their very own child. There was no way I could have coped on my own, and Mary had always said how lovely it would be to have a sister for Peter. I just thought . . . I thought I had done the right thing. At the time, I didn't know if we would ever have a life together.'

She looked around, but nobody had anything to say, so she continued.

'It was three months later that you left hospital, and you know the rest. We got married and came to start a new life here in France. We wanted to put the past behind us. It was easy for me to drop out of sight. Oh, I know how much Mary helped me, but our family was never particularly close-knit. I told her only to get in touch with me if it was an emergency.

'I did say I thought she ought to tell Leanna on her eighteenth birthday she had been adopted. I thought by then she would be adult enough to understand why I did what I did, and perhaps forgive me. I didn't take into account Mary not living to tell her. She was so much younger than me, and I knew she would keep her word. I've been on tenterhooks for the past four years, wondering if or when Leanna would want to find us.'

'So you weren't ever going to tell me I had a daughter?'

Bel looked down at her hands and shook her head. 'At the time I thought it was for the best. You can't miss what you've never had.' She looked up again, at each of them, imploringly. 'If only I could have my life back I would do everything differently, I promise you, but I can't, can I? All I can say is I'm terribly sorry for the upset I have caused, but at the time I thought I was doing everything for the best. I would have loved to have kept you, Leanna, really I would, but I couldn't. I just couldn't.' She started to cry.

Harry and Alex were staring at each other, stunned into silence. Leanna felt it was time she should say something.

'I do understand, Bel. And Mary and Ted were wonderful to me, you know. I had a very happy childhood.' After a pause, she went on, 'I was fifteen when I discovered I was adopted, and at first, I didn't want to know. But then I became curious. I had no relatives that I knew of, and felt terribly lonely. It was purely a stunning coincidence I met Alex and we put two and two together. I'm not here to make trouble, I promise you.' She didn't know what else to say, so sat back with a sigh.

'That's very charitable of you, my dear,' said Harry. 'I am appalled about what has happened, but I must say I am absolutely thrilled to learn I have a daughter. It'll take a while before it all sinks in, I'm sure. Now then Bel, we're not being very hospitable. How about we all have a drink to celebrate?'

Bel wiped her eyes and immediately leaped to her feet. She went to get a bottle of wine from the pantry and glasses from the sideboard.

'Well,' chuckled Alex, 'you've never had a birthday present like this before!'

Harry nodded, lost for words.

Bel opened a cake tin and proceeded

to cut up a large fruit cake and hand it round. She looked a little happier now that she had something to do.

'Talking about coincidences, Alex, you couldn't have come at a better time,' Harry said, giving the fire an aggressive poke.

'How's that?'

Harry looked pointedly at Bel. 'She needs an operation and is loath to leave me on my own. I can cope perfectly well of course, but she insists I can't. It will mean travelling to England, but it won't be for long.'

Alex looked from one to the other and grinned. 'So you'll have to come back home at last. Mum and Dad will be pleased.'

Harry pulled a face. 'In view of this latest development, perhaps it is time we came home.' Turning to Leanna, he said, 'We haven't heard your story yet, Leanna. I don't know if you feel like relating your sequence of events, do you?'

11

Alex and Leanna were to have returned on the early morning ferry, staying overnight at a motel near the port, but Harry implored them to stay at least overnight.

'We have a small single bed Leanna can have, and Alex, you can have the sofa here. You'll have to share it with the cat, I'm afraid.'

Although Leanna would have liked the chance to discuss it privately with Alex, there really didn't seem anything she could say, other than that she would be happy to stay. She hoped Alex didn't mind. After all, it would seem rather strange dropping such a bombshell, then leaving quite so soon. Still, Leanna felt awkward, especially as she was to be given a room to herself.

Leanna didn't sleep very much, but she doubted if any of them did. It had been such a bewildering day for all concerned and yet, she thought, she was glad she had come. At least now she knew why she had been adopted and could well understand how Bel must have felt all those years ago. She thought about Philip, wondering what he would say when she told him of her experiences. She'd had quite an adventure, and it wasn't over yet.

★　★　★

'Are you sure you don't mind staying on?' Alex asked Leanna the next morning. They had been given the job of feeding the chickens and it had given them time alone for a while. 'I promised you'd be back in your campervan in a couple of days, but in the circumstances . . . Harry can manage very well, you know. A damned sight better than me at times. Don't be fooled by the wheelchair. As you can see, though, Bel likes to mother him.'

'It's all right. Bel will feel happier if

there's someone here. I understand. And besides, there's a lot to do packing everything up. I can make myself useful in that department.'

'I can't believe they're finally coming back to Whitby,' Alex said. 'You certainly have a way of making things happen, don't you? My parents have wanted them to live nearer for the past twenty years.'

'Not my doing,' she said, with a shrug. 'Just another of those coincidences.'

'You talked Bel into having the operation, too. You're a miracle worker, my girl.'

'It'll be nice to spend some time with my father,' she said, with a smile of happiness. It was nice to be appreciated. 'Will you do me a favour though? Go and see Joe at the campsite and explain. He'll wonder where I've got to. You can also tell him I've found my real parents. I know he'll be pleased. He's been so helpful and kind. If it hadn't been for him, I wouldn't have got this far.'

'Of course I'll do that. You're a brick, you know that? You have taken all this in your stride, much more than anyone could have expected of you. I am completely amazed.'

She sighed. 'Harry and Bel are nice people. I don't want any unpleasantness. I don't think it has sunk in yet, all the ramifications, but I am glad you persuaded me to come. Truly I am.'

Alex squeezed her arm affectionately. 'I've already rung my parents and told them about Harry and Bel returning, so they can get on with seeking suitable accommodation for them. It won't be a problem, and there's plenty of space at the family home to start with. The sooner we get Bel fixed up with a hospital appointment, the better.'

'She is going to be all right, isn't she?' Leanna asked, with a worried frown.

'Of course she is. Leave it all to Uncle Alex,' he added, with a wry grin.

She laughed. She still couldn't get over Alex being her uncle.

* * *

Before Alex and Bel left for Whitby, Bel took Leanna to one side. She looked apprehensive.

'I didn't want to say this in front of Harry and Alex, but it's something I think you ought to know. Mary and I fell out over Ted. I met Ted first and fell in love with him, but as soon as he saw Mary, that was it. He had eyes for nobody else. At the time, I blamed Mary for luring him away from me — which, of course, was utter nonsense, I realise that now. But at the time I was furious. I vowed never to speak to her ever again. I had my own flat and my career, so we went our separate ways. Then I met Harry and knew we were made for each other. We had so much in common.

'We decided to get married within a month of meeting, but Harry knew his folks were going to be a problem. You know the sort of thing — *you can't possibly know after only a month*, and

159

all that. Anyway, he was going back to spend Christmas with them and tell them when he thought the time was right, only of course, it didn't happen. He had the accident and spent Christmas in hospital. It was touch and go if he survived, like I said. Then he spent most of the following year in and out of hospital. I hardly ever saw him. I don't like to be reminded of those times, but I was at my wits' end. Part of the reason I've been putting off this operation is because I have an absolute horror of hospitals now.

'When I discovered I was pregnant, I felt so alone, and so frightened. I couldn't tell his parents, they scared me to death. They still do,' she said, pulling a face. 'My own parents were dead, so there was only Mary I could turn to. She was married to Ted by then, and they had already adopted Peter. I knew they wanted another baby, and when I told them I was pregnant, but couldn't keep the baby, they instantly offered to have you. I think I knew they would. I suppose, in my own stupid way, I thought it made sense for Ted to become your father, as he was my first love.

'I know it sounds as if I am making excuses, but I can't change what happened, no matter how much I wish I could — oh, you can't imagine the times I'd wished things could have been different! But once I'd let Mary and Ted have you, I felt I had to stay out of your life. I am sorry, though. Truly sorry, to have missed seeing you growing up. I always wanted a large family, but it was not to be. Harry and I have just each other.'

Leanna gave a gentle smile. 'Thank you for explaining. Like I said, I didn't want to cause trouble, I was mainly just curious. Although now, I am delighted to have a family to which I belong. My in-laws have been wonderful, but it's still not the same as a proper family, is it?'

Bel gave her a hug. 'Bless you. Thank you,' she whispered. 'If I can, I would like to make it up to you. I'm just so sorry Ted and Mary and Peter aren't still around. It must have been a dreadful time for you. Once we all get back to Whitby, perhaps we can meet your husband too and have a proper family get together?'

'Yes, I'd like that.'

* * *

Leanna and Harry spent the next few days packing belongings into boxes, and finding homes for the animals. Leanna felt awkward to begin with. She didn't know what to call Harry. 'Father', or any of its derivatives, seemed sort of uncomfortable, so she was pleased when he suggested she call him Harry, like everyone else. He was a quiet individual, thoughtful and intuitive, so they soon felt at ease with one another. Eventually, they even felt comfortable enough to tease each other.

Harry did seem genuinely horrified at what Bel had done, so Leanna did her best to placate him. She was surprised at how easily she herself had accepted the situation. As the days passed, she found great pleasure in learning about Harry and Bel's life, realising now why she was attracted to the arts. Harry still painted, sufficient to make a comfortable living he told her, and Bel was a freelance writer. She'd had several short stories and articles accepted for publication, and was working on a book about the French Revolution.

★   ★   ★

Two weeks later, Alex arrived in a large van to collect them, and gave them the good news that Bel had been seen promptly at a private hospital, had the operation, and was recovering well.

'She's nattering on about you both though, so the sooner we get you packed up and away, the better,' he said, gazing round at the miscellaneous heaps.

'Leanna has worked miracles,' Harry told him. 'I don't know how I've managed all these years without a daughter.'

Leanna blushed. 'It's been a joint effort, Harry. Actually, I've quite enjoyed it, but it will be nice to get back. I think Harry's looking forward to going home too,' she told Alex. 'Nervous maybe, but pleased all the same.'

'What about you, Leanna? Keen to return to York?'

Leanna smiled. 'Of course I'm dying to tell Philip all my news, but I still want to complete my challenge, so I've another two weeks before I can go home. Think you can put up with me that long?'

'No problem at all. We shall all be sorry when it's time for you to leave. I'm sure Harry feels the same, but fortunately you won't be far away.'

* * *

Back in Whitby, Alex reluctantly dropped Leanna off at the campervan.

'Are you sure we can't twist your arm

to come stay at the family home? My parents are dying to meet you.'

'No, I think they have enough to cope with at the moment. But I would like to meet them before I return to York, if that can be arranged.'

She said good bye to Harry and went in search of Joe.

12

'Why was I called Leanna?' was the first thing she asked Bel when they next met. It was something that had puzzled her all her life, as she had never met or heard of anyone else called Leanna.

Bel smiled. 'Harry's middle name is Lee and my name is really Annabel, so I joined the two names together and came up with Leanna.'

'Oh, of course. How clever.'

'I thought it would help trace you later, if it ever became necessary, if you had an unusual Christian name.'

The meeting with the elderly Graysons went well. They made Leanna very welcome, and since they knew York quite well they found plenty to talk about. They expressed a wish for Leanna to bring her husband to meet them next time she visited. Leanna agreed to do so, but suppressed a grin, thinking about Philip's aversion to Whitby traffic.

★ ★ ★

Leanna trundled back to York early one morning. The weather was cold with a nip in the air, but fortunately no snow. She pulled up outside their home mid-morning with a huge sigh of relief and satisfaction. As expected, the house was deserted, but surprisingly tidy and to her great astonishment, in the hall was a beautifully decorated Christmas tree. Entering the kitchen, she was further surprised to find the refrigerator well stocked and a gorgeous bouquet of flowers in the middle of the breakfast bar. A card attached from Philip said welcome home, and sorry he wasn't there to meet her, but he had an appointment he had to keep and he would back as soon as he possibly could.

Leanna felt overwhelmed and relieved. She was sure everything was going to be all right now. After a quick look round she set about unpacking and preparing for when Philip returned. She rang his mother to thank her for taking such good care of things in her absence. She could tell Enid had obviously been looking after the housework; Phil couldn't have managed on his own. Enid was overjoyed to hear from her and they spent a happy while chatting.

As soon as she heard Philip's key in the lock she rushed to greet him. He dropped his briefcase and hugged her so tightly she feared her ribs would break.

'I've missed you so much,' they both said, and laughed.

'I have got so much to tell you,' she said, dabbing tears from her eyes.

'So have I,' replied Philip. Holding her at arm's length, he added, 'But first I want you to promise you'll never, ever, do anything like that again. I've been worried sick.'

She gave him another hug. 'I promise. Now can we go and sit down. I'm dying to know what's been happening while I've been away. I gather from your mother that your dad's been poorly.'

It took them most of the day to each relate their experiences of the past four months. When Philip learned she had met her real parents, he was both shocked and delighted.

Once they were cuddled up in bed, Leanna said shyly, 'I have another confession to make, darling. I'm not sure how to tell you this, but I hope you'll be pleased. You see, I believe . . . although I'm not absolutely sure, I haven't seen a doctor or anything, but . . . I think I'm pregnant.'

'Darling, why haven't you seen a doctor?' Philip asked anxiously. 'Are you all right? How does it feel? Oh my goodness, that's marvellous news.'

'So you don't mind?' she said, sounding greatly relieved.

'Darling Leanna, I'm thrilled! And Mum and Dad will be over the moon. I can't believe it — I'm going to be father. How do you know? How sure are you?'

'I did a pregnancy test a couple of months ago, and it was positive. I so wanted you to know straight away, but there was never anyone here when I rang. I must say I was rather miffed and a little bit cross with you,' she said, teasingly annoyed.

He kissed her tenderly. 'Sorry, my love, but I was all at sixes and sevens, what with you being missing and Dad being poorly. There was a lot to do. I did leave various voicemail messages, but I guess you wouldn't have accessed those.'

'I'm sorry I misjudged you, sweet-heart.'

He chuckled. 'So when is Junior due?'

'I reckon about Easter.'

'Wow. I say, how do you feel about having a party to let everyone know you're back? Wait until the gang hear our news.'

'I'd be delighted. I can't wait to see their faces when they have to tip up a £100 each. Also, I want you to meet my folks.'

As they snuggled up in bed, Philip said, 'With all the joy of having you back, I forgot to wish you a belated happy birthday, darling.'

'Thank you,' she said.

He lay back, smiling happily. 'We can go and collect your present early tomorrow.'

'Collect it? From where? What is it?'

'You'll have to be patient. I think we've had enough excitement for one day, don't you?'

* * *

The next day they set off to visit Philip's parents, where they were expected for lunch. As soon as they were in the house Philip said she had to close her eyes. She laughed as he led her through to the kitchen and placed a cardboard box in her hands.

'You can open your eyes now,' he chuckled.

She stared at the box, puzzled and then lifted the lid cautiously.

'She's gorgeous,' she cried with delight, seeing the tiny, squirming puppy inside. 'What a little cutie. You couldn't have bought me anything nicer. Thank you so much. I feel quite emotional.'

He gave her hug. 'I realise I've been an idiot, but it's all going to change now I'm to become a family man. With your help, Leanna. I can't ever imagine life without you.'

'And I can't imagine life without you, sweetheart. I realised that soon after I left. I do love you so.'

* * *

Leanna and Philip had a quiet family Christmas with his parents. Leanna was pampered and fussed over by all. It did feel good to be back. Their friends were organising a party for New Year and Leanna agreed it would be fun to attend, although not for long as she couldn't drink now and she didn't want to be a party pooper. She was looking forward to seeing their faces as she recounted her adventure. Philip told her they were stunned she had taken the challenge seriously.

On New Year's Eve she dressed in a new maternity smock that Philip had bought her and recalled the last party she had been to at Henry and Josie's.

'It'll be a while before I can slip into a little black dress again,' she said to Philip as he hunted for his socks. He turned and walked over, kissing her lovingly.

'You look simply marvellous. Radiant, I believe the expression is. How is Junior behaving? You're sure you feel up to going tonight? We could always cancel.'

She laughed. 'I wouldn't miss it for the world. I don't suppose we'll be on their guest list much longer, shall we? I can't imagine any of them happy to see the destruction one little pup can do, and that's before the baby makes his appearance. But it's what makes this a home isn't it?' She watched anxiously as Philip turned to see what the puppy had found to play with. It was one of his socks that he had intended wearing. Instead of getting angry like he would have done previously, he chuckled and threw the pup the matching sock rolled up in a ball.

★ ★ ★

Leanna was embarrassed by the attention she received when they arrived at Henry and Josie's bungalow. They had decided to be socially late, turning up when the party was in full swing. Even so, they were soon the centre of interest, as Leanna laughingly demanded her challenge money.

'If we had gone to the police I don't think you would have got away with it,' Henry said, smiling as he handed over his £100. 'But I think you deserve it all the same.'

'Hear, hear,' agreed Jerry, taking out his wallet. 'Can't see Tania lasting so long on so little. Well done. Come on, George, get your money out,' he said, giving George a slap on the back.

'£100 I think we said, didn't we?' George reluctantly handed her a cheque. 'Henry's right though, we should have contacted the police. Security cameras everywhere, you would have soon been picked up.'

Damian was the last, and chuckled as he handed over his contribution. 'Whatever did you do all the time you were away? With no television and so little to occupy yourself it must have been awfully lonely.'

'Not at all,' replied Leanna. 'I wrote a book about the whole experience. I'm hoping it's going to be a bestseller.'

A little later, after she had chatted to the men's wives she went in search of Philip. As she approached, she overheard him explaining about her father and saying he thought they may be putting the house on the market. Walking home arm in arm she asked him if he was serious.

'Of course, sweetheart. When your folks visit they'll need a room on the ground floor won't they? Besides, I think it would be best if we found a place nearer to the works, somewhere more suitable. I fancy a dormer bungalow with a large garden, what do you think?'

'Sounds wonderful. I'm looking forward to you meeting my parents and the rest of the Graysons tomorrow, although I must say I am a bit anxious. They don't know I'm pregnant yet.'

'They will be as thrilled as I am, I'm sure.'

'What shall I do with all this money? In a way Henry was right, I would soon have been discovered if you had contacted the police. These days, even if you don't use a credit card, you're monitored everywhere. I would probably have been stopped at customs when I went to France, for instance.'

'I think you should spend it on yourself, my love. You proved to that lot back there you don't have to spend a lot to enjoy yourself, but you certainly deserve the chance to treat yourself.

From what you've told me, on the whole you did quite enjoy the experience.'

'Yes,' she said, ruefully, 'I did most of the time, but it would have been so much nicer if you had been there too.' She found she really meant it. 'I've been thinking, and I'd like to take my mother out shopping. The Graysons are quite wealthy and I thought Bel might like to have some new clothes to make her feel more at home. What do you think?'

'It's a lovely gesture and I heartily approve. And perhaps when you sell your manuscript you can take me out shopping, too,' he added, with a grin.

We do hope that you have enjoyed reading this large print book.

Did you know that all of our titles are available for purchase?

We publish a wide range of high quality large print books including:
Romances, Mysteries, Classics
General Fiction
Non Fiction and Westerns

Special interest titles available in large print are:
The Little Oxford Dictionary
Music Book, Song Book
Hymn Book, Service Book

Also available from us courtesy of Oxford University Press:
Young Readers' Dictionary
(large print edition)
Young Readers' Thesaurus
(large print edition)

For further information or a free brochure, please contact us at:
Ulverscroft Large Print Books Ltd.,
The Green, Bradgate Road, Anstey,
Leicester, LE7 7FU, England.
Tel: (00 44) **0116 236 4325**
Fax: (00 44) **0116 234 0205**